The characters and events portrayed in this book are fictitious. Any similarity to real persons, living or dead, is coincidental and not intended by the author.

ISBN-13 (Print): 979-8-9863022-2-5

ISBN-13 (eBook): 979-8-9863022-3-2

Edited by: Sheeba Arif

Cover design by: Chloe Arzuaga

Disclaimer

Please be advised.

The stories in this collection are works of fiction, and the events in each story are not necessarily based on actual events. These stories depict, to various degrees, actions that may be hard to read about, including physical violence, emotional abuse, supernatural terror, suicide, and other sensitive topics. While these themes may be difficult for some readers, I believe there is something to learn from them.

I am solely responsible for any errors, misrepresentations, or offenses.

I hope you enjoy the following stories.

With love and respect,

Besu Tadesse

Broken Persons

A Collection of Short Stories

Besu Tadesse

Sankah Sankah

"I can't believe you."

Tracy was chastising Darren for his recklessness. "I can't believe you're still sleeping with her." That night, it was his decision to engage in a casual romantic relationship with a young lady he had met at a bar three months prior. Since then, they had met regularly but never without being intoxicated to some degree, and for only one reason.

"I can't believe you keep bothering me about it."

"It's even weirder that she has the same name as me."

"That's not true—her name's different."

"Does she go by some name other than Tracy?"

"Yeah, but she spells it with an 'e'."

"How would you even know that? Are you writing love notes now?"

"Of course not. That's how she saved her name in my phone. And that's how she introduced herself."

"What?" Tracy could not hide the contempt in her voice.

"Yeah, she stumbled over to me, stuck her hand out with a firm handshake, and said, 'Hi, my name is Tracey-with-an-'e'—with an "e".' It was really funny."

"Jesus, Darren."

A loud explosion came from the television in the dimly lit living room where Darren was playing video games. "I don't know what to tell you."

"Whatever. When is she coming over?" Tracy was tired and both her questions and answers were getting shorter.

"Whenever she texts me, I guess. I should have about ten minutes from then."

"Alright, well, I wish you good times. I'm going to get some sleep. I have an early morning."

"Ok, sounds good. I'll hit you up tomorrow to figure out the plan for next week."

"Sure. Talk to you next week."

"Alright, bye!" Darren slid his phone from his ear to end the call but found that Tracy had ended the call first.

Darren continued playing his game for a few moments until he saw a text message pop up from his phone in a bright glow and a loud ping. It was Tracey-with-an-'e'. He did not bother reading the text. He knew he had ten minutes to get ready.

He turned the game off and swept his hand over the couch to remove any questionable laundry. *Is this clean or dirty?* Darren grabbed a shirt and sniffed it, trying to decipher the general cleanliness. He decided not to take any chances and just go with the plain gray T-shirt he was already wearing. *This is fine, the minimum is enough.* He walked from his front door to his bedroom to make sure there was nothing on the floor. No accidents, no hiccups. They both knew the routine, and he wanted everything to be as smooth as possible..

He went to the kitchen to clean the counters and give the appearance that he was not just doing this for Tracey-with-an-'e'. Doing that risked signaling to her that she was someone special. There was a fine line between maintaining everything well enough in his apartment to avoid scaring her away from disgust and displaying any effort that would scare her away through a fear of commitment. He never wanted any serious romantic relationships, and it took him years to figure out the right balance.

He was going to give his microwave a once-over and wipe the inside when there was a knock at the front door. He hurried out of the kitchen and took a sip of his beer sitting on a table. *My God, how long has that been there?* Then, he quickly straightened out his shirt and walked to the door. He never had much company, so there was no need to look through the peephole—*just open the door.* In walked Tracey-with-an-'e', wearing a charcoal-gray jacket, blue sleeveless top, a skirt that shimmered like a disco ball, and chunky black heels that clopped along the apartment floor.

"Hey." She kept conversation to a minimum.

"Hey."

She went to put her purse and jacket on the couch. "Sorry, I was at this happy hour for work and I lost track of time."

"It's ok, I've just been here playing vi—"

Before Darren could finish, she had turned around and shoved her tongue in his mouth. He grabbed her waist as they sloppily kissed each other. Their hands roamed across each other's bodies without much rhyme or reason. After a few seconds, she grabbed his hand and aggressively pulled him to the bedroom without much resistance.

Minutes later, they were on the bed—two sweaty, panting masses staring at the ceiling.

"Geez, twenty minutes? You must have missed me. I have to start being late more often."

Darren was mildly annoyed. "It's probably because you didn't reek of cigarettes this time."

"Or probably because you actually cleaned up a bit and feel good about yourself." *Damn, she noticed*, he thought. "Don't worry, it's a good thing. No one's falling in love here. Just glad you made some kind of effort. Most guys I hook up with usually don't even bother to wear a clean shirt." As she spoke, she rolled out of bed to look for her clothes.

"Thanks, I guess."

"No, the pleasure was all mine." She had already hooked her bra and slid on her skirt. "Did you see where my top went?"

"I think so." Darren swung his feet to the floor and walked to the foot of the bed where he remembered throwing her blue top earlier. He dug through a pile of clothes on the floor that he pulled from the laundry the previous night and found her top mixed in. He also found a pair of athletic shorts, which he put on after tossing the top back to Tracey-with-an-'e'.

"Here you go."

"Thanks. I'll probably be around the area tomorrow night, too, if you want me to come over."

Darren was cheeky. "Sure, I don't mind you... coming again."

Tracey-with-an-'e' rolled her eyes. "You know, I'm starting to question why I keep..." She hesitated, so as not to encourage his corny adolescent humor, "... returning."

"I don't know either, but it's a good time. You know the drill, just text me." He went back to the bed and laid down, this time spreading across the entire bed.

"Alright." She walked out the bedroom door and he was already half asleep. She put her heels on and grabbed her jacket and purse. Then Tracey-with-an-'e' went to a small drawer in the kitchen and pulled out a key, engraved with the words "Home Sweet Home" in fanciful red letters. She took the key and walked out the front door, locking the door behind her. She slid the key under the door, far enough so it was not reachable from outside, then stumbled toward the elevator and left the building. Darren was asleep before she even pressed the elevator button.

Darren struggled to wake up the next morning. *That beer must have been out for a while after all.* He stumbled out of bed, shirtless and wearing the musty red shorts from the previous night. He felt beads of cold sweat dripping down his back. He remembered seeing two bright, glowing yellow circles, floating as if they were sitting right above his eyes. *What was I dreaming?* He searched the floor for the cleanest shirt, a plain blue T-shirt with a small coffee stain from his late-night working session two nights before. Putting on his shirt, he walked out of the room and straight to the front door. He retrieved his apartment key from the floor and returned it to the kitchen drawer.

He bent down to the freezer to search for a frozen breakfast item. *Waffles? No, I had that yesterday. Oh, there's a breakfast burrito.* He took the burrito from the freezer door and unwrapped it. He folded the burrito into a paper towel before placing it onto the single clean plate in his kitchen. He opened his microwave to see splattered sauces and crust inside. Wincing briefly, he put the plate with the burrito in the microwave and set it to cook. *I need to do something about that.*

While he waited for his burrito to cook, he put on his slippers and went to the basement. There were some video games that he wanted to play that day, and he had stowed them in a plastic bin in his storage unit. He walked into the storage area and flipped the light switch, but the light was out again. He stumbled in the dark until he found his unit. Remembering the feel of his lock, he entered his combination and yanked it open. He tapped his fingers around until he found the bin with the games, then slowly pulled it out, trying to avoid scraping his skin against the old metal links in the unit door. He placed the lock back on his unit and was backing away through the darkness when he bumped into something. It felt like a person was standing behind him. He quickly turned around only to see more darkness, a shock running through his body. There was no one there.

"Hello?" He waited a few seconds, but no one responded. "If someone is down here, sorry I bumped into you. I'll be more careful." Still, no one answered. He shuffled his feet a bit to make sure that there were no other objects around him. Not finding any other impediments, he walked to the exit. "Okay, I'm going to lock up now. Hope to see you around." He closed the door behind him, not seeing the bright, glowing yellow eyes staring at him from just across the room as he walked out.

He went back to his apartment and put one of the old video games into his console. While it booted, he went to the microwave to retrieve his burrito. The smell of old sauce mingled with the aroma of cheese and sausage. He tried to ignore the smell. "I gotta do something about that mess in the microwave."

He juggled his plate to the couch so that he could eat while starting another daylong gaming session. Settling into his favorite spot, he picked up the burrito and tenderly peeled back the soft, soggy paper towel. Going for a bite, he heard a faint, breathy whisper in his ear:

"Sankah sankah..."

He stopped, eyes wide and jaw clenched. He turned around and shifted his eyes around the room. "Who said that?"

There was no response. He stretched his body over the top of the couch to look around, too lazy to turn his whole body and check in earnest. Still nothing.

He felt anxious, but there was nothing and no one in the apartment. He went to take another bite.

"Sankah sankah..."

This time, a cold hand gently gripped around his throat.

He jumped up screaming, the burrito flying out of his hand and the plate flipping off the couch and onto the table. The sound of the plate hitting the table startled Darren again, and he jumped, flying over the back of the couch and landing on the ground. He fell hard against his left knee and shoulder. He winced in pain, not understanding what had just happened. He grabbed his throat with his right hand, checking for any signs of pressure, scratch marks, anything that could help him understand. To his surprise, there was nothing. Even the temperature of his neck felt normal.

Darren pulled himself up into a cross-legged position and checked his leg and shoulder. They hurt, but he did not feel any breaks or dislocations. Still, he knew that he needed to patch himself up, and he was overdue to buy a first aid kit anyway. Between that and the mess in the microwave, he realized it was time for a trip to the market. He put on a pair of black sweatpants and a light jacket and went to the supermarket across the parking lot to pick up supplies.

Darren hobbled to the supermarket, trembling slightly with anxiety. *What was that? Am I going crazy?* He could not get out of his mind the feeling of a cold hand against his neck. He chuckled to himself about the plate scaring him, but he wanted to make sure that he was not having any other issues. He had not been back to the market in a long time, preferring to have his meals delivered to him. He lived in a high-rent area and spent so much on delivery that he did not have much in disposable income for going out, even to catch a bus or a train to watch free events. Playing video games and recycling the same old hookups from his college days was easier and cheaper.

The market had been rearranged since the last time he was there, so he had no idea where anything was anymore. He grabbed a basket and slowly made his way near the pharmacy to pick up a first aid kit, then he walked to cleaning supplies to get sanitizing wipes for the mess in his microwave. He also wanted snacks for his gaming session, so he made his way to the "snacks" aisle, wincing along the way. He walked back and forth until he found what he wanted—the last two bags of chocolate frosted donuts. But when he reached for the bags, his hands went numb and cold. The feeling also moved to his feet and ankles. It was the same icy restraint that gripped his throat earlier. He heard the voice in his ear again.

"Sankah sankah... "

He turned to his left to see a shadowy child-like figure, staring at him from six feet away. Its eyes were glowing and yellow, shining brightly in the harsh supermarket lights, and the edge of the shadow was shifting, as if the figure was moving back and forth against its own outline. Darren blinked long and slowly, then looked around to see if anyone else had noticed. There was no one else around. He tried to speak.

"What—"

Before he could say anything else, the shadow had grown and moved toward him rapidly, obscuring his surroundings as the icy grip clung tighter around his wrists.

Darren turned and ran in the opposite direction, screaming uncontrollably. When he got to the back of the store, he turned sharply and tried to push his legs as fast as possible. However, just as he reached the back of the store, his left knee buckled, and he fell hard again, this time on the linoleum market floor, near a stacked bread display. People around him stared as he lay on the ground, trying not to scream again in pain from the fall. A store manager appeared from the back room.

"Sir, are you okay? Is there something that we can do to help?" Rather than being angry, the manager was very reassuring.

Darren was surprised, and the manager's calmness helped him relax. "Yeah, sorry about that. I thought I saw someone that I didn't want to see. I'm okay, though." He tried to get up on his own, but the manager insisted on helping him up.

"Do you need us to do anything? We have some forms you can fill out to address any liability, and to give us suggestions on how we can improve."

"Oh, no thank you, I don't plan on suing anyone, and the store is fine. But I did leave my basket in the snack aisle, and I'm having a hard time. Can you help me get it?"

"Sir, stay right here. I will get your things for you."

The manager started walking away to get Darren's things.

Darren called out, "Thank you. It's the blue basket with the first aid kit and the wipes." The manager signaled with a thumbs-up. Darren considered asking for the donuts, but since that seemed to be the cause of his situation, he refrained.

Darren thanked the manager for bringing his basket and for being so nice. "If there's anything else we can do, let us know how we can help." With that, the store manager went back to the office to continue working.

Darren was still hungry. He found himself near the bakery, which was also not far from the produce area. He grabbed a short loaf of wheat bread, then walked over to the produce section for apples, oranges, a package of diced pineapples, broccoli, lettuce, and carrots. They were all small and easy to lift and carry, and he did not want to take any more chances to see the weird shadow thing in the rest of the store. Thankfully, he did not have any more encounters. He shuffled to the self-checkout aisle to pay for his items, then he placed them in plastic bags and walked back to his apartment.

Darren's body hurt too much from so many falls that day, so he was not up for cooking or cleaning when he got home. He was, however, in the mood for romance. So he called Tracey-with-an-'e' to see if she was available that night. She was, again, in the area for a working session, and they were going to take a break and regroup later. She would be there in less than five minutes.

He was not expecting her to be available so soon, but he could not back out. So he put on a brave face, iced his knee, quickly applied some disinfectant spray to a few scraped areas, and patiently waited on the couch.

Tracey-with-an-'e' knocked on his door approximately three minutes later, then turned the knob to no avail. Darren had inadvertently locked the door on the way in, as he had not initially considered contacting Tracey-with-an-'e'. He lifted himself from the couch and opened the front door for her.

"Locked? That's new."

"Sorry, I just had an accident earlier and..."

"Yeah, I'm sure that was rough." She had moved past him, both physically and conversationally. "I have a few minutes until everyone needs to get back, and we have a big presentation due. Let's do it." She immediately started kissing and grabbing him.

Darren tried to slow things down. "Hey, this is great, but be gentle. I hurt my knee earlier."

Tracey-with-an-'e' gave him a smug look. "I mean, I don't usually do gentle, but I'll try." She led him back to his bedroom.

He lay on the bed, clothes halfway off. Tracey-with-an-'e' was already down to her underwear. She started kissing his neck and the exposed part of his chest, as she desperately tried to remove the rest of his clothes. She moved to his abdominal area, kissing further down his body. However, just as she attempted to remove his pants, he felt the icy grasp around his stomach, crotch, and thighs. Darren looked up to see the shadow, poised behind Tracey-with-an-'e' in such a way that he could see only its head, shining yellow eyes staring deeply into his. The eerie coldness radiated to his fingers and toes. He heard the whisper again.

"Sankah sankah... "

Instinctively, he dug his feet into the bed and pushed himself back, slamming his back into the wall and holding back his screams. Tracey-with-an-'e' was startled.

"What? Did I do something wrong?" She leaned up, her eyes big and her mouth agape.

The sweat on Darren's skin was a combination of romance and terror. "Huh? No, you didn't do anything wrong. Sorry, I think it was just a muscle thing."

"Ah, ok," Tracey-with-an-'e' said seductively. "I think I can do something about that." She pulled Darren back onto the bed, and Darren complied. She finally removed his pants, kissing around his legs and midsection, teasing him while he kept his eyes closed. He was enjoying the moment and did not want to see the shadow again. He tried to ignore the chill creeping over his body again, refusing to make a sound, refusing to show any reaction to the physical stress and anxiety. The feeling was unbearable, especially as Tracey-with-an-'e' became more intense, more passionate. All of Darren's nerve endings were firing, leaving him unable to distinguish between pleasure and pain. Writhing in anguish and unable to bear it any longer, he opened his eyes for a split second. That was all it took. The shadow appeared mere inches from his face, glowing yellow eyes shining brighter than before, searing into his soul, the sound of long, labored breath filling his ear.

"Sankah... sankah..."

The few seconds Darren screamed felt like an eternity. He backed into the wall behind him so hard that you could hear the large thud in the apartment hallway. He pushed so hard that he was almost standing straight up on his bed, wearing only a shirt. Tracey-with-an-'e' pushed herself away, off the bed and stood fully up. She was still in her underwear, stunned and embarrassed.

"What was that?"

Darren did not have an answer for her. His sweat was now fully cold on his skin, and his legs felt like toothpicks. "I... I don't know."

Tracey-with-an-'e' went from stunned and embarrassed, to frustrated and irate.

"You know, if you didn't want to do this, you shouldn't have texted me."

"No! It's not that. I don't know what's going on. I want to do this."

"Well that's fine for you, but now I don't want this. Not like this." She quickly put her pants and sweatshirt back on. "I'm not saying I want to stop doing this, because it's fun. But something's going on today, and I really can't do this right now." She walked out of the bedroom. Darren followed her, upset but understanding. If he went to her place and she started acting the way he was acting, he would want to leave too.

She put on her jacket and grabbed her purse. "Just, call me when you're feeling like yourself." She hurriedly kissed him on the cheek and walked out. "I need to get back to work. Don't feel bad, I'll talk to you soon."

Darren stood in his living room, upset, and scared. *Am I really losing it?* He grabbed a pair of mesh athletic shorts lodged in between the cushions of his couch, which he kept for such emergencies. The pain in his knee and shoulder were creeping back and his ego was crushed. But most of all, his nerves were scattered. He tried to drink water and sit quietly on the couch, with no change. He tried to lie on the couch, eyes closed. That only made the anxiety worse. He did push-ups and sit-ups, ran in place, stretched his legs as best as he could. Fighting through any pain that he had from before. That made him feel better, but not fast enough.

Darren was scared, and sad. He felt vulnerable, like he was floating in the very darkness that he had seen around the brightness of the shadow's shining eyes. He was not sure what to do. It was not a feeling he understood, the feeling of isolation, his mind and eyes playing tricks on him. And he was not used to feeling so helpless, to know that whatever he was trying to do was not relieving him of the pain. By separating himself from any real connection or responsibility outside his basic life, he had numbed himself to even the idea of pain, let alone the feeling of it. But now, he needed to reach out. He called his one consistent friend—Tracy. Without the "e".

Tracy came to Darren's apartment an hour later, after finishing a home project. She had not been to his apartment for some time but was happy to see that her spare key to his place still worked. When she walked in, the apartment was in worse shape than she remembered, and Darren was lying on the couch with pillows elevating his left knee.

"Geez, what happened here? What happened to you?"

Darren choked up as he saw her. "Tracy, I need help."

Tracy was taken aback. "Darren, what's going on? Did something happen?"

"I'm not sure. I'm not really ready to talk about it. I just wanted you to come by."

"Of course, Darren." She took off her jacket, put her purse down, and pushed his coffee table back so that she could sit on the floor next to him. "Want to hear about what's been going on with me?" Darren nodded.

Tracy told him about the work that she was doing in the house. She was replacing curtain rods and curtains with more modern styles, upgrading light bulbs, and changing some switches to smart, eco-friendly models. She was also gearing up for promotion season at her firm, which entailed a grueling process of interviews, slideshow presentations explaining why she was ready to move to the next level, soliciting letters of recommendation, and general schmoozing about which she was not excited. Darren listened, letting her words sink in. *She is so ambitious, so focused. She takes herself so seriously.* She spoke with such passion about her work without being boring, making everything seem relatable and important. Though she spoke long, it felt like mere minutes.

"So that's all that's going on with me. What about you?"

Darren, on the contrary, did not have much to report.

"Well, I was planning to play some games, but I ended up tripping and hurting myself. Then I tripped again when I went to the market to get supplies to fix myself from the first fall. Then, I came home, started getting anxious, and then I called you." He avoided saying that Tracey-with-an-'e' was there earlier that day, and he certainly did not want to talk about a child shadow chasing him everywhere he went.

"That's messed up. But I'm glad you called. We haven't hung out in person in so long." She stretched to look up at the kitchen. "By the way, I didn't get a chance to eat yet. I'm assuming you don't have any real food. Is there a place you want to order from?

"Actually, I have food."

Tracy's eyes widened in surprise. "Wait, what? You have *FOOD* food? Or do you mean those chocolate frosted donuts you like? Those don't count."

"No, smart-ass. I mean actual food. I picked some up while I was at the market."

Tracy stood up and walked to the kitchen. She saw plastic bags filled with bread, fruit, and vegetables. "Well, well, well. Look who finally showed up to adulthood." Darren wanted to be offended, but she was right. "This is actually a pretty good start. I can make a salad with this, which could make for a nice, light meal. And if you're feeling anxious like you're saying, it's probably best to keep the belly light tonight."

Without hesitating, Tracy started finding utensils, washing lettuce and carrots, and chopping fruit. In minutes, she had assembled two bowls of salad, complete with sliced lettuce, carrots, apples, and diced pineapples. She left orange slices on the side of each bowl and served each with a tall glass of water.

"Sorry there wasn't much to work with, and I didn't feel like going back to the market. I can bring you some more food tomorrow if you'd like."

Darren felt gratitude welling inside him. *How had I never seen this side of her before? Was it always there?* He ate with Tracy and talked about the recent games he had played. He told her all about the stories and control schemes, and the histories of the studios that developed them. He talked about the themes and how they worked or did not work with the gameplay. He explained the drama behind how certain games were developed and released. He immersed her in a story that she had not heard, and she admired his commitment to understanding the industry and the craft.

"This is really impressive, Darren. Why don't you do anything with this?"

"What do you mean?"

"You know so much about this stuff. Maybe you could start a blog about it."

"I could, but that takes a lot of effort. I really only have time to play and think about gaming. My day job takes up all my other time."

"Well, if you had someone that could invest, maybe this could become a full-time thing. Or at least a paid part-time thing. Then you could afford groceries and maybe come to my place to hang out for a while." Tracy said the last part with a little more flirtation than she expected. Darren noticed, and he smiled at the thought.

"That would be nice. But where would I find someone to invest?"

"Well, I know some people with money that might want to help. At least, as a favor to me. And I could throw a little money in there."

"Oh no, I couldn't. It would be weird."

"Not for me. I charge interest." She smiled even harder.

Darren laughed. "Okay, if you plan on charging interest and helping me find people to invest, maybe I can give it a real shot."

"It's a deal." Tracy reached out her hand to shake his. Darren lifted himself up to shake her hand in agreement. They smiled and looked at each other. Darren had not realized how supportive she was, nor how beautiful.

The next several years of dating and eventual marriage between Darren and Tracy were blissful. Tracy moved up in her career, becoming the Chief Financial Officer at her company, Darren settled into his life as a stay-at-home father while working on his gaming blog. It was not much for him yet, but he had never been happier. They had friends, security for themselves and their family, and their sweet infant son Ellis. Each day, Darren saw little changes—a new wrinkle in his skin, thinner or graying hair on his head or in his beard, some dryness around the knuckles. He embraced everything with Tracy. He had lived a healthier lifestyle ever since making their relationship official. Eating better, sleeping more, drinking water, keeping the kitchen clean, and even learning how to cook for himself and his family. Life was wonderful.

"Hey Dee, I'm about to head out." Tracy grabbed a hot breakfast sandwich from the microwave while balancing her laptop backpack and purse

Darren was walking out of their bedroom with Ellis and a bottle of formula. "Sure thing. Don't forget to take your salad, too." He pointed to a pre-made salad sitting on the kitchen counter.

"Thanks, honey."

"No problem." They gave each other a peck on the lips.

"I may be home a bit late. I hope that's okay."

"Again, not a problem. Ellis and I have plans to watch some live streams anyway."

"Okay, but not too late. He needs his sleep."

"I know. I need my sleep, too." They smiled at each other and Tracy walked out the front door of their apartment. Darren followed behind to make sure the door was locked.

As he held Ellis in his arms to feed him, he thought about that old apartment he lived in before, when he was still single. Crusty carpet, shabby walls, and his mind always scattered. He thought about his new life and how much better it had been. He felt more vibrant, more focused, more motivated to pursue the things that he loved. His living area was certainly cleaner. And he knew that, while she never brought it up or threw it in his face, Tracy was the one that helped him realize this new life.

He sat down on the couch to turn on a gaming stream—research for his blog—and to get some ideas about games that he would like to design someday. He spotted a pink box sitting on the living room table, and he realized that there were some cupcakes that their neighbors brought over the night before. Darren, Tracy, and Ellis had just moved in only a couple of weeks prior, and the neighbors were kind enough to bring sweet treats and baby supplies for the family to enjoy and use.

Using one arm to balance the baby, Darren reached over and lifted the lid to the box. There was still a whole large cupcake, with thick chocolate frosting, sitting in the center. His mouth started to water. He had not eaten all morning. He remembered that he had made a plate for himself – eggs, and toast with a side of fresh fruit – just as she used to make for him when they were dating.

"I should eat the plate I made."

But the plate is all the way in the kitchen.

"Meh, I can eat that later. I can take at least one bite of this cupcake."

It's just one bite. I can work it off later today.

He reached into the box to grab the cupcake. His palm and fingers came away covered with dollops of frosting. He turned the cupcake over to grab the paper liner for better grip and went for a bite. Just then, he felt a swift, cold sensation run across his face. The shock knocked the cupcake out of his hand and onto the floor. The cupcake fell and rolled onto its side, leaving a chocolate cream stain on the new carpet. Confused, he looked at baby Ellis, whose body started to feel colder. Ellis turned his head to look at Darren, his still-developing neck becoming stronger and more stable, the whites of his eyes going dark as his pupils glowed a bright and shining yellow. Darren felt his old anxiety from years ago creeping up again. He could not tear his eyes from his child and what he was turning into.

A dark shadow engulfed Ellis as he spoke his first words.

"Sankah... sankah..."

Lullaby

"Over my dead body!"

Mikael spent another night trying to convince his mother to let him study music. "Mom, I hate this. I hate it here. I hate being in Pennsylvania. I don't like any of my classes except the music ones."

"I don't care! I'm spending all of this money to send you to school. You're not going to do this to me." His mother's breath became heavier and more labored as her anger increased.

Mikael was desperate. "What is the problem? I told you this is what I wanted to do, and I said I was willing to try something else. It's not working, and my grades in my other classes are not as good."

"That's because you decided to get lazy. You're not even trying."

"I'm trying every day! Mathematics is not what I want to do."

His mother was flippant. "Then do something else. You're just not going to do music."

"I don't want to do anything else!"

Mikael's mother dropped any façade of empathy. "Look, I didn't work my entire life for you to waste your time. I'm not going to let you do this to the family or to me."

"So this is about you?"

"No, that's not what I meant."

"But you just said—"

"Mikael!" She yelled his name hard to make him stop talking. She always yelled like that when she felt like she was losing control of the conversation. Mikael complied, and they both listened to each other breathing as they tried to compose themselves. His mother spoke first. "Mickey, I've said this before already. I love you, and I don't want you to regret this decision."

Mikael hated when she called him "Mickey," especially when they were fighting. He never felt it was out of affection, only to manipulate him to calm down so that she could dominate the conversation again.

"You just said this was for you."

"Mickey, it's for you too. I don't want you to struggle."

Mikael took a few deep breaths to calm his nerves, then he found a way to calm his voice. "Look, I have a project to finish and I have exams next week, so I need to study."

His mother conceded for now. "Okay, I will let you go. I love you."

Mikael grunted, "Okay."

"Mickey!"

Reflexively, he relented. "I love you too."

"Okay, I will call you tomorrow."

"Fine, bye." He went to touch the "End Call" button on his phone.

His mother let out a "goodbye," which he heard just before he ended the call. He was mad, mad that his mother could make him feel worthless. Helpless. Like he had no one there supporting him. He had his friends, and some of his teachers were fond of him, but without his mother on his side, holding him up during harder times, what good was any of it? He sat on his bed and sobbed for a few moments.

"Hey Mickey, are you coming?" Teddy called from the living room. Mikael quickly wiped away his tears, took two deep breaths, straightened his clothes, and walked out of his bedroom.

Teddy was sitting on the couch with a movie paused on the television. "Are you ready to watch? I heard this movie is good."

"Oh, I don't know. I need to finish this project for my digital production class."

"You sure? I was waiting for you?" Teddy was picking at a large bowl of buttered popcorn.

Mikael considered the proposal. "I mean, we can start the movie at least. It's not due for a few days, and I got most of it done. I should have some time." He grabbed an unopened bottle of water from the kitchen, then went to sit on the couch near Teddy. "What are we watching?"

"I don't know. I just picked 'What Should I Watch?' and went with whatever came up."

"Sounds good to me. You know how much I care." Mikael sat on the couch and grabbed a handful of popcorn from the bowl.

"You talk to your mom again?"

"Yeah."

"She still hates you doing music?"

"Yeah."

Teddy winced. "Yikes, sorry man. Parents are the worst."

"I know somewhere she means well, but I don't think she's listening to me."

"My parents don't listen either." Teddy scooped more popcorn into his hand and picked individual pieces into his mouth.

"Yeah, but at least you're pre-law. It's something they can get behind."

"Are you for real? I just told my dad that I was going to be a lawyer. He looked at me and said, 'Son, why would you do that? Don't you know how volatile it is? Why can't you just be a doctor?'." He quoted his father with an exaggerated accent. "It doesn't matter. When they're miserable, nothing is going to make them happy. You might as well just do what you want and keep it moving."

"I hear you, but she's paying for the degree. I can't really do much." He took a sip of water, then he shoved a large handful of popcorn in his mouth.

"Sure you can. You can get a job on campus or ask some friends for money. Not me, though, I don't have much, but probably some other friends."

They both chuckled. Mikael was still reserved in his laughter. "Teddy, you know I'm not asking you for money. You never have any."

"This is true. If you paid for everything in the apartment, you wouldn't have money either." Teddy gave a wry smile.

"Hey!" Mikael feigned a shocked expression. "It's all good, I'll figure it out."

"That's fine, but you really need to get some real help. This has been going on for a while, and it's starting to get to you."

Mikael started patting himself down, as if trying to find the problem on his body. "Is it? I don't think I feel any different."

"Come on, I'm serious. I can see a dark cloud over you every time you finish talking to your mom. But every time you do something you care about, it's like you're a completely different person. I'm not saying you need to stop talking to her *completely*, but I think you need a break from her."

"So, here's the problem." Mikael bent forward and started animating his hands. "If I don't call her, she *blows* up my phone. Last week, I didn't call her one night, and she called me *seven* times while I took a twenty-minute nap the next day."

"Did you tell her that it's a problem?"

"Of course I did."

Teddy leaned his head toward Mikael, to reiterate his question. "But, did you *really* tell her?"

Mikael reiterated. "I *really* told her. I told her that it was bothering me, and that it hurt me. Then one day I yelled at her to stop. That worked for about three days. Then she got back to doing it again. It's bad, but this is the only way to keep things from becoming worse."

Teddy leaned back in his spot on the couch. "Man, that sucks. I'm sorry. My stuff isn't that bad."

"Like I said, it's ok. I'll figure something out."

The movie had been playing in the background, a low-budget romantic comedy about rival lawyers–turned–lovers in a small town during the Christmas holiday. The male protagonist's quick-witted friend spewed another one-liner. "There's only one place for a lawyer to find an official lady for the holidays—the bar."

Mikael had heard enough. "Nope, I don't have the time for this one today." He grabbed a final handful of popcorn and his water. "I'm going to go finish that music project." He stood up and walked to his bedroom. "You gonna keep watching?"

"Yeah, man. Will they or won't they? I need to find out, will or won't."

"Okay man, I'll see you in the morning."

"Wait, before you go to bed, can you water the plants on the balcony? I forgot to do it earlier today."

"Yeah, I'll do it right now."

"Thanks, man."

"No problem. Good night."

"Good night! Good luck, man."

Mikael opened the sliding glass door to the balcony and poured some water from his bottle into the various pots. The weather was unseasonably warm, so Mikael and Teddy maintained a small garden—they had some small vines and other plants. It made for a pleasant view for passersby too. Most students did not bother with décor, so their apartment was always noticeable.

After watering their little garden, Mikael walked back to his room and closed the door.

What is this place?

How did I end up in this alley? Oh, I'm behind the apartment building. Did I finish my project? Why am I not asleep? I have a lot to do tomorrow, I shouldn't be down here.

Why is it so dark? Who would come down here? Why am I here? I really need to get back and rest. This project is getting to me.

Wait, who is that? That looks like Mom.

Oh God, it's Mom. Mom, why are you here? I thought you were back home in Virginia. We need to get you upstairs.

Hey Mom, thanks for coming, but you shouldn't be here. Take my hand, we need to go upstairs.

Wait, Mom, why are you letting go? It's not safe here. We could get really hurt.

Who is pulling on me? Mom, are they with you? Mom! Someone is trying to take me! Get help!

Stop, don't push me towards them! What is this? There are sirens going off everywhere and they're choking me! Stop it! Mom! Stop! Stop!

Mikael jolted awake, the world violently shaking before him.

"Mickey! Wake up!" Teddy was standing over Mikael, shaking him vigorously by his collar. "You need to get up. You have your differential equations final in thirty minutes. Isn't the final halfway across campus? Hurry up!"

He was right. It took twenty minutes to get to the testing site from the apartment. Not a lot of time to get dressed, eat breakfast, and get there in time to settle in and prepare. Mikael shot up quickly in his bed, still breathless from the nightmare he had had.

"Hey Teddy, thanks."

"No problem." Teddy accepted the thanks as he turned and walked out of the bedroom.

Mikael swung his feet over the edge of the bed and hurriedly grabbed a pair of socks from his top drawer. Then he slipped on a stained hoodie from his desk chair. No time to change into proper clothes. Black and red holiday pajamas would do. It was not the first time this had happened.

He breezed through the living room, grabbing his backpack and stepping into his sneakers in smooth motions. He secured the backpack tightly over his shoulders and dug his heels into his shoes so that he did not have to lace them again. They were uncomfortable, but he figured he could fix them once he arrived at the exam.

"Alright, man, I'm out."

Teddy sat on the couch with a large plastic bowl. His mouth was crammed with cereal while he held up another spoonful, waiting for the chance to shovel it in. "Alright, I'll see you later."

Mikael swung the door upon and swiftly walked out the front door.

Later that night, Mikael was on the phone, again with his mother.

"I think I figured out what I plan to do with graduate school in a couple of years."

"Mickey, why don't you ever do the video call? I would like to see your face sometimes."

"Mom, focus."

"Oh . . . okay. What were you saying?"

Mikael sighed and rolled his eyes. "I know what I plan to do for graduate school."

"Oh really? I hope you've been listening to me."

He closed his eyes and took a deep breath. *It's always about her.*

"I'm going to do music engineering."

There was silence on the phone for about five seconds. "Mom, did you hear me?"

"Yes, I heard you."

"Oh, just wanted to make sure. So, there's a graduate program called music engineering, which is part electrical engineering and part digital production. That way, I can still learn some of the engineering things without stopping my music stuff. I think it's a good compromise."

There was more silence. Mikael waited several moments for his mother to respond.

"So, do you know how you're going to pay for it?"

Mikael was stunned. "What do you mean? When we talked about grad school a few months ago, you said you would help me with whatever I wanted to do."

"I don't remember saying that."

He was doubly stunned, his jaw dropped. "Hold on, hold on. We *just* talked about this. You even said that you set aside some money, so long as I went to grad school right after I finished here. It's what you always said. You promised. You don't remember?"

His mother hesitated. "Maybe I said something like that, I don't know."

Mikael became stern. "No, no. This is important. I need to know the truth. You said that you would support whatever I would do, and that you were available for what I needed. Do you remember that—yes or no?"

More hesitation. "Look, Mickey, I'm not going to support this. Maybe I said something before, but I'm telling you, you're not going to do music with my money. You can do whatever you want to do, but I didn't agree to anything like that."

She had done this before. Every time Mikael's attempted to hold his mother accountable for something that became inconvenient for her, she claimed that she did not remember, or that she would never have said such a thing. Once, she had agreed to take him anywhere he wanted to on a Saturday afternoon in front of his father. Later, he had secured an audition for the countywide band for that same day. She claimed that she had never agreed to take him to an audition, but in a rare show of authority, his father backed him up. He inferred that was why all his conversations with his mother from then on were one-on-one—to make sure there were no witnesses. He also inferred that was part of the reason they stopped getting along.

"Don't do that, Mom. You know what you said."

"Don't tell me what I said. I think you aren't remembering it correctly."

"Of course you would say that. You never remember anything you say. That's fine, I will figure it out myself."

His mother was irritated, and you could hear it in her voice. "Mickey, don't talk to me like—"

"Goodbye, Mom."

She took a moment to reset her temperament. "Okay, I will talk to you soon. I love you."

He dryly repeated himself, "Goodbye, Mom."

She repeated with emphasis, to compel him to repeat it. "Mickey? I love you."

He repeated it one final time. "Goodbye, Mom."

"I love—"

He hung up before she could finish.

"Teddy, I'm finally done." Mikael stormed to the living room couch, huffing and stomping his feet. He slumped onto the couch, shifting pillows to get comfortable. "I'm so tired of my mother disrespecting me. I need to get some money and a new place. I've got this year and next year, then I can just go do my thing, but I don't think I can take anymore." Eyes welling, hands shaking, stomach turning in on itself—

Mikael choked back tears. He hated feeling this way. He was at a breaking point. All the denial, all the gaslighting, all the subtle bullying and her trying control his life, and not just for his college choices. She tried to control or manipulate his every decision. She overly scrutinized his every statement, twisted everything to fit her own agenda. He had finally hit his breaking point.

He looked up to see what Teddy thought, except he was not there. There was a young woman, another student, sitting in his spot on the couch. "Hello."

"Oh my goodness, I'm so sorry. I didn't mean to do that."

"It's okay, I should have said something." She reached out for a handshake. "I'm Miriam."

He reached back. "I'm Mikael. Do you know where Teddy is?"

"He is taking a call on the balcony. Are you ok?"

Mikael blushed from embarrassment. "Yeah, it's fine. I've just been going through a thing."

"It sounds like your mom is being awful. So is mine. Have you gone to the campus health center? They have counselors you can talk to."

"I haven't. Someone told me about that, but I don't feel very comfortable talking to people about my problems."

"Well, I was just there last week. I have a lot of issues with them stressing me out all the time."

"Has it helped?"

"It didn't help them stop being awful. But it did help me deal with my other problems so that I could manage stuff better."

"What do you mean?"

"There is a lot of competition at this school, and everyone is so anxious and stressed. Plus, I was always a bit socially awkward, and I've never been able to reach out and make friends with anyone. I ended up being alone a lot when I was in high school. It just took a lot out of me. I finally had a breakdown and cried in the middle of campus freshman year. After that, I walked over to the health center and scheduled a meeting. It really helped me. But like I said, it doesn't help the people around you become better. It just helps you become better at dealing with things yourself."

Mikael thought about it for a second. Miriam's last statement hit home for him. *Become better at dealing with things yourself.* That's exactly what he needed, to deal with things himself.

He needed a plan, and he needed someone or something to help him get on the right path.

"You know, no one has ever put it to me like that. Once I get done with this final project for music production, I'll find out more information for next semester."

"Nice! I hope it works out."

Teddy walked into the apartment from the balcony and slid the glass door shut. "Hey Miriam," he said, before seeing Mikael on the couch. "Oh, hey Mickey. Good to see you." He turned back to Miriam. "You ready?"

"Sure." She stood up and turned back to Mikael. "Nice meeting you. I hope you find the help you need." She turned away from him and walked to Teddy's room with him. They locked the door behind them and did not turn the lights on.

Mikael was elated. Someone had given him a leg up, a way to at least try to manage the problems he was dealing with every day. He was filled with new motivation to complete his music project. He went back to his room, turned on his computer, and spent the next two hours working. He completed it just before midnight. He turned off his electronics, including his computer and his phone. He knew he did not have any finals or obligations the next day, so he was safe to sleep in. He stripped down to his boxer shorts, slid into bed, curled into his sheets and blanket, and fell asleep to the faint sounds of his own breathing and Teddy's bed squeaking back and forth.

I'm choking. I'm drowning.

Wait, I'm drowning. Where did all this water come from?

Hands are pushing me down. Pushing me forward? The pressure on my chest is releasing. They're pushing me up, faster and faster.

I'm out! I hit the ground hard, but at least I'm breathing. It feels like sand under me.

How did I get to the beach? I was just at the apartment. Look at all these people around.

Help! Help! Why doesn't anyone hear me? I thought I was screaming. My mouth doesn't feel like it's moving. I can't even hear myself scream.

Everyone seems like they're fading away. Help! That just makes people fade away faster. Even the beach feels like it's shrinking. It's getting foggier around me. I can't see as much distance as I did a few seconds ago.

I'm alone on this beach. I need to get away from this place.

There is some driftwood. How did that get there? Was it always here? Never mind that now. I need to build a raft. No rope or twine, though. Wait, there's some rope in my pocket, tied in a noose, and it's dry. How did it stay dry in my pocket? How did it even fit in my pocket? The rest of me is . . . wait, I'm not wet anymore.

No time to think about it. Need to focus. This driftwood is very solid, and this rope is strong. I finally got something going.

Alright, a little more pull here. Perfect, it's secure. I still need a sail. I'll just use my shirt. Has my shirt always been this big? Let's tie this as a sail.

Okay, let's see if it holds.

Looks like it's holding. I don't have much time. I need to get home. This raft is sturdy. I'm surprised I was able to build this. I'm not even that good of a swimmer. I did pass my swim test. I should be okay for a little while.

This water is warm. Very warm. And the sun is bright, but not too bright. This feels like freedom. Like I can just be out here by myself forever. There's a warmth, the ocean embraces me, cradles me from below. I haven't felt this feeling since . . . ever.

There's land up ahead. A different land. The sky above that shore is somehow even bluer than the last. How long have I been floating out here? It feels like it's been forever, but also hardly any time at all.

I'm starting to accelerate. Am I sinking? It's the hands again. They've come from the water. Please don't take me back into that darkness. I don't think I can be in there again.

The hands grab the raft. This is it for me. I won't make it to shore.

The hands, they're . . . pushing me forward? It was the hands accelerating my raft. I'm moving closer and closer to land again. Why are they helping? Did they snatch me away so that I could find this place? There could have been a better way. The shadow hands could have just bought me a plane ticket or something.

The raft is picking up speed. The wind is refreshing.

Now, more speed. The wind is less refreshing.

Even more speed. The wind is moving so fast, I'm finding it harder to exhale. I need to turn my head to catch my breath.

I can sense the water growing shallower. I need to brace myself or I'm going to fly off the raft.

We're coming in too fast. I'm going to—

———————————————

Mikael woke up, rolled, and fell off the couch. He hit his head on his desk and landed with a thud on the floor.

"Ow!" The pain settled into his head immediately. His chest and pants were soaked. He tapped his fingers to his crotch to check if he urinated, something that happened if he had too much to drink but not normal on a completely sober night. "Ugh . . . " He sniffed his fingers. "Alright, it's just sweat." He stood up, wincing from the pain, and walked back to his room to get aspirin from his desk drawer. He tossed two pills into his mouth and drank water from the previous night's bottle. Then, he laid back down on his bed until the aspirin kicked in.

While he waited for his headache to subside, he thought about his dreams from the last two nights. Other dreams he had were either extremely vague or focused on something baser. Dancing at a party, trying to hook up with a classmate, playing music, or something else that he was trying to do in the real world. But these two dreams were darker and more ambiguous. Mikael was not a spiritual person, unlike the rest of his family, so he did not want to put much stock in them. Still, he felt there was some force pulling him in the direction he was supposed to go. Or maybe there was something more troubling. How did he end up on the couch? Why was he so sweaty?

He thought that he should get a sleep study. It would be easy to figure out at the health center when he went to find a counselor for the following semester.

Once his headache had slackened, he took a shower, changed his clothes, and went to the health center. The staff nurses said that they could get him a referral for a sleep doctor in Virginia while he was on winter break, or he could get someone when he came back. He also scheduled an appointment early in the semester with a counselor and reached out to a career advisor on how to make his transition from mathematics to music engineering. He would have to take a few additional courses to make up for missed requirements, but fortunately he could catch up with an extra class in the spring and two remote classes during the summer. Without much else to do, he went back to his apartment to have lunch and watch a movie. About an hour into the movie, he fell asleep on the couch with a belly full of cereal and a smile on his face.

Mikael was truly hopeful. There was finally a plan for his future. He had never felt closer to freedom.

Later that day, Mikael was sitting on the couch, watching a trashy reality show. He had submitted his final project for his music production class earlier in the day. He had also written a plan for how he would get the help he needed. He had one final exam for his differential equations class, which he was not worried about. Despite his disdain for being a mathematics major, his grades were always good.

While he lay on the couch, watching a screaming woman throw a cocktail in a man's face, his phone started buzzing.

"Ugh, again?" He picked up the phone. Another call from his mother. "Nope, not today."

He watched for another two minutes. Another buzz from his phone. He picked up the phone again. Another call from his mother. This went on for another fifteen minutes before she let up, long enough for another episode of the show to start.

Five minutes after that, another buzz on the phone. He noticed seven text messages from his mother. There was also one more call—this time, it was his father. "Seriously?" His father called him only after his mother bothered him to call. Knowing that his mother would not leave his father alone, he called his father back.

"Hello?"

"Yes, Dad. What do you need?"

"Hi, son. I was just calling to see how you were doing."

Mikael stayed quiet.

"Mickey, are you there?"

Mikael sighed heavily. "Yes, Dad. What do you need?"

"Look, son, your mother just wanted to make sure that you were okay."

"I'm okay."

"Okay. I don't want to bother you."

"I know."

"I love you, son. And your mother loves you, too."

"Yeah, I know." Mikael knew his father would not force him to say it back. "Just try to call a little more."

"I will."

"Okay. Bye, son."

"Bye." He ended the call and put his phone on the table. The buzzing stopped.

Mikael stayed on that couch all through the day and night. His brain slowed as time passed, and he enjoyed every minute. The longstanding pressure on his shoulders and chest had been lifted, the air felt easier to breathe, the fog in his mind cleared. Each moment felt better than the last, and he wanted to savor it. Mikael knew that it would not last. He knew that his job prospects may not be great, and that he would need to hustle if he wanted to ensure a good life for himself. But that was tomorrow's problem. Today was a day of joy, and he was not going to let anything interrupt this feeling. He closed his eyes and basked in the promise of freedom.

I'm back on the beach. I made it to this new island. Is it an island?

The sand here is finer. The trees are more lush. There are towels and umbrellas everywhere. There are people here. This must have been where everyone went. Where is everyone?

Oh, there's a path to the left with footsteps. Let me go over there. This sand feels great under my feet.

Where are my shoes? Did I bring my shoes? Who cares, I can go get them later.

There's too much fog in front of me. Can't see anything. The fog feels warm. I've never felt warm fog. I can feel the path switching from sand to wood. Must be entering the boardwalk.

Now the path is switching from wood to stone. Is there a stone version of a boardwalk? I guess it would be a sidewalk. I'm not sure what I'm feeling.

The fog is dissipating. What is that sound? Is that rain? No, it's a . . . crowd. Where is the crowd coming from? Wait, this is a party!

Am I the featured DJ? They're calling me over to the booth. The booth looks like a really cool cage, and there are flowers all around it. What a cool concept.

Everyone is so excited to be here! What's that track playing? Oh wow, it's my final project. It is such a big hit. I'm filled with joy again.

They're calling me to stage dive. I've never done that before. Should I do it? The crowd looks so far down.

I'm going to do it! These spotlights are bright and hot. The noise is getting louder. It's so exciting!

Teddy? What are you doing behind me? I'm so happy to see you! I can't hear you, but . . . "Go, go!" Thanks so much for being here, and for your encouragement. I'm ready.

I jump into the crowd. I'm floating over the crowd. I can feel their energy. So much support, so much love. This is the moment I've been waiting for, the feeling of acceptance. Finally, I've found people that really understand me. I'm so excited that I can hardly catch my breath. My hands and feet feel so cool, and the air is sensational. I close my eyes and take in all the joy.

Mikael's lifeless body lay across the street in front the apartment building, among the cries from late-night onlookers and emergency medical technicians rushing in vain to save him. After several minutes, they placed his body in a bag and loaded him into the ambulance. Teddy told the police that his friend walked in his sleep to the balcony, slid the door open, and balanced himself on the edge of the railing. He started to scream, "No!" repeatedly, but Mikael had just smiled, eyes still closed, and let himself go. He told the authorities about the last few days—fights with his mother, sleeping at all hours, feeling depressed and isolated. That same morning, Teddy saw him asleep on the couch as he left for the day. Mikael never liked sleeping on that couch and would never do so if could avoid it. His story was consistent with what the authorities saw. They thanked Teddy for his statement and asked for his family's contact information to notify them, which they promptly did, despite Teddy's insistence that he tell them later that night. He did not want to tell people of a loved one's death until they have had a good meal and a place to sit, but that was not protocol.

It was the last day of final exams. All exams were cancelled. The fate of many students' grades left in flux until the new semester. Some made insensitive comments about this, but most were respectful and sympathetic, even offered to contribute financially towards the inevitable fundraiser.

Since his body was found on a Thursday, and because of the nature of the incident, the local funeral home extended assistance to Mikael's surviving family to do a quick, small ceremony over the weekend. Since the weather was mild, travel from Virginia was easy. Mikael's parents attended, as well as a few friends that were allowed to extend their stay on campus. Some were able to get special exemptions to stay in their dorm rooms until after the ceremony. Others lived like Teddy, in apartments off-campus. Teddy stayed to help manage logistics for Mikael's family.

The ceremony was well-organized and had little fanfare. The funeral home contacted another home in Virginia to receive the body for a more proper ceremony among his loved ones that could not attend. Among the people that eulogized Mikael were Teddy and a few classmates that knew Mikael well. Then one professor came and spoke, his music production teacher.

"Good afternoon." His voice was deep and soothing. "My name is Dr. Ernest Logan, and I was Mikael's music production teacher." He shuffled a few papers and took out a pair of reading glasses. "My apologies, I wasn't sure if I would be able to attend and if so, if I would be able to do this. But I will try my best."

He straightened his papers nervously.

"Mikael was a rare student. He was not majoring in music, but he had a passion which rivaled any of his other classmates. He didn't know all the theory or how to write every piece that he recorded, but his work was vibrant and full of life, bursting with emotion and thought, and he could put it all together with such ease. He had a gift, a natural talent that I have only seen maybe once or twice in all my years of teaching. He didn't speak much in class, but when he did, it was with such warmth and grace. He could tell you any story, no matter how simple or mundane, and it felt so soothing—like hearing a prayer." Dr. Logan's voice trembled slightly as he spoke, and he wiped a single tear from the corner of his eye.

"I don't want to take up too much time. I know this is supposed to be short. I just . . . I wish I got the chance to see him realize his full potential. To see what he could give to the world."

A small electronic sound echoed through the room. It was a speaker system turning on.

"I did ask with the permission of the funeral home if I could play an excerpt from his final project, which he sent me this past week." Tactfully, he did not mention that it was just hours before his life ended.. "While I haven't translated everything that he used, I was assured by his friend Teddy that there was nothing in the music that was graphic or offensive." He smiled at Teddy, who acknowledged Dr. Logan silently. "Not that I ever knew Mikael to write such music." Mikael's mother glared at Dr. Logan, a mixture of grief over her loss and disgust at the man she thought was coercing him into being a musician.

"Anyhow, here is his final piece for my class, entitled, 'The Dream of Ruth.' I hope you enjoy it."

Ruth. Mikael's mother's name.

The music started softly, with a dancing flute melody against a synthesizer sound. Slowly, the sound of hand drums rose in the background, volume increasing gradually. The music built in strength over ten seconds, with stringed instruments and more flutes joining in. Then the music suddenly dropped, leaving only the synthesizer sound. A sample started to play with the music. A young woman was singing as a baby cried in the background. She sang the same words over and over again.

"Esheruu-ruu-ruu. Esheruu-ruu-ruu." Hush, hush.

Ruth's eyes widened, then she started weeping uncontrollably. She knew the song because it was an Ethiopian lullaby. She knew the woman's voice because it was hers.

She was transported back to the day it was recorded. It was the first time that baby Mikael was really sick. Not just sniffles or a small fever, but really ill. He had a high fever and had been throwing up. His parents tried everything to get him to relax. Even the medicine they gave him did not seem to work. They called the doctor, but he was overwhelmed with other cases of other infants. Eventually, Mikael's parents got their baby to drink and hold down some juice. In desperation, a young Ruth took her child in her arms and started singing to him, "Esheruu-ruu-ruu, lijeh, lijeh." Hush, hush, my baby. His father grabbed a video recorder, hard to come by in those days, and started recording. She was annoyed that he would think of recording at a time like that, but he wanted to capture the moment. She sang for several minutes, until little Mikael went to sleep. His fever came down, and when he woke up, he was back to his smiling self.

Ruth remembered her son being home for Thanksgiving and rifling through the VHS tapes in the basement. That must have been what he was looking for, the recording of that moment. She and her husband had played that tape several times for Mikael as he was growing up. He must have remembered it. She thought he had forgotten all about it. She thought he forgot all about her.

Ruth wept, listening to her own voice singing to her now-lost son, hoping that she could find peace one day. Hoping that he was finally at rest.

The Grand Tour

"This is simply amazing."

Herman Montgomery stepped out of the pod after travelling through space for what seemed like an eternity. He looked around his landing area, lush and green with all types of colorful plants that he had never seen before.

"Truly remarkable. What a delight to come back to Earth after so long. I told everyone things would be okay when we came back."

He tried to spot any signs of human life, but there was nothing to be found. So he stepped out of the chamber and walked down the retracted steps to the soil below. He was so happy to be out of that cramped pod, surrounded only by cold chambers and electronic gadgets. Finally, fresh air and real, sentient life.

He touched the grass and trees and was sniffing a yellow flower nearby when he heard the clopping of hoofs in the distance. They were coming closer and louder, just beyond the tree line to his right. He walked through the trees to find a beaten path. There were several thin tracks crisscrossing through the dirt. To his left, he could see a horse-drawn carriage approaching him. The carriage had a simple yet elegant design, with gold embellishments and bright green and red accents against its white exterior. The windows were covered with light cotton cloth, and the horses pulling the carriage were tall, strong, and brown with coats that shone as brightly as the carriage itself. As the carriage drew closer to Montgomery, he saw flecks of gold dancing in the horses' manes.

He stepped back from the path to allow the carriage to pull next to him. He looked up at the carriage driver, who wore a white cotton tunic with white pants, brown sandals with several straps crisscrossing his foot, and a white cotton scarf with blue trim, which he wrapped around his neck and head. The carriage driver tugged the reins gently and the horses stopped at the exact point which brought the carriage door directly in front of him. He could see someone's silhouette facing forward, still and unwavering, but he could not make out its face. Just then, the carriage driver turned around and spoke through a small slot behind him.

"*Sayidati*, we are ready."

The silhouette moved from the seat and turned towards the carriage door. The driver leapt down from his seat and took out a stepstool from a small compartment next to him. The stepstool was made of pewter, simple and sturdy, and the driver pulled rods from beneath the stool to provide more stability.

After pulling out the rods, he placed the stepstool beneath the door to allow his occupant to step out and introduce herself. She was beautiful, and she wore a cotton dress with basic designs woven on her cuffs and collar. Her eyes were big, and her hair was wrapped in a cotton shawl, with only a single black curl hanging from the front of the wrap.

"Hello. My name is Charlotte Marroquin. Welcome home, Mr. Montgomery." She moved to one side and politely gestured to Montgomery to step in, slowing nodding in affirmation that this was real.

Without thinking, he stepped carefully from the pewter stepstool into the carriage, mouth agape and legs still a bit wobbly. Once he secured his seat, Charlotte followed him back into the carriage just as effortlessly as she exited, while the carriage operator collected himself and climbed on. Montgomery could not believe what he was hearing. She knew who he was. But how? *Surely, I've been gone for a long time. And she appears so young. Did they just keep pictures of us around? We must have been remembered well. Are we really that legendary?*

He sat across from Charlotte, facing front in the direction of the carriage operator. Charlotte sat in her previous seat.

"It really is a pleasure to meet you, Mr. Montgomery. We don't usually have people return here in the Maghreb."

"The Maghreb. So, we're in North Africa?"

"Oh, Mr. Montgomery, we—"

"Please, call me Herman."

Charlotte tilted her head slightly, thrown off by the informality. "My apologies, but we do not speak so informally to a man of your stature. If it doesn't bother you, I would like to continue referring to you with your proper title."

Montgomery was impressed. *Just like my subordinates.* He pondered for a moment. "Okay, that is fine with me."

"Mr. Montgomery, the term 'Africa' really doesn't apply anymore. What your generation referred to as 'continents' have changed quite a lot, and as such, we have organized ourselves differently."

He looked outside to see farmers tilling the soil and children running around, picking and smelling the colorful flowers blooming everywhere. "Ah, I see. Well, times change, I guess." He chuckled nervously. "How did this become so green and lush?"

Charlotte opened her hand with her palm facing up, revealing a small electronic device.

The device emitted a blue glow that displayed a three-dimensional picture of Earth. She displayed this fluidly, as if she had given this speech a thousand times before.

"In short, the climate crisis from many generations ago led to an event known by many names. *Al Enheyar Al Aadham, Le Grand Effondrement.* But you would have probably referred to it as 'The Great Collapse.' When the Collapse occurred, over several decades, many people died. Not millions, but billions. Across most of the planet, there was famine, disease, wars due to migration, water shortages, which led to large-scale population reduction. These incidents led to people simply not having as many children, reducing our planet's population even further." As she told the story, the Earth hologram rotated, showing hurricanes and tsunamis, tiny blue dots sweeping back and forth, then suddenly turning red and fading from the display. Large areas changed colors, from green to brown, to gray, to black. For the Maghreb, the colors moved from brown to green. "We were one of the fortunate few."

Montgomery only heard snippets of the story but was impressed by how far technology had come. While he understood the broad historical strokes, he maintained his focus on the device in Charlotte's hand and the colors dancing back and forth in front of him. "This technology is amazing. I had only seen things like this in the movies."

"Is that right? I think there was much inspiration from your films and other media that led to the development of the display glove."

"Truly remarkable." He stared at the farmers in the fields again and saw that some had the same glove—tracking weather patterns, reading to their children as they worked the land, seeing people talk to their loved ones in real time and real space. "Say, is there a way I could get something like that?"

"I'm sure that we can figure something out for you, Mr. Montgomery."

"That would be wonderful. I have to ask though. Is there a way to get something... more elegant?"

Charlotte was curious. "More elegant, Mr. Montgomery?"

"Yeah, elegant. You know, something like this could display directly in front of you from your eyes. Imagine being able to open up your display with just your thoughts and have the display move dynamically. Or how about, you can see your friends when you call them, in space, as if they were right in front of you? Wouldn't that be something?"

Charlotte relaxed and smiled. "Why yes, that would be something amazing, wouldn't it? I will speak to my associates when we pick them up for the trip. As a matter of fact, here is one right now."

The carriage slowed to a stop next to large and beefy man holding a gold-plated staff taller than him. As he stepped into the carriage, he slammed the staff into the ground. The staff retracted into a tube that fit in the palm of his hand. He did not require the stepstool, rather, he simply stepped into the carriage and hooked the retracted staff onto a little notch on his belt.

"Mr. Montgomery, please meet François Khoury."

François had a smooth, deep voice. "Mr. Montgomery, it is a pleasure." He extended his arm for a handshake. "I hope our society has been treating you well thus far."

Montgomery shook François's hand. "The pleasure is mine. And yes, Charlotte has been telling me all that has happened while I was away."

François turned to Charlotte. "Has he been informed of *Al Enheyar Al Aadham*?"

"Yes, he has."

"Have you spoken about the event tonight?"

"Not yet, François. I promise we will in a moment."

"My apologies, *Sayidati*. I'm just very excited. We haven't had such a Grand Tour in several years."

"*Pas de problème*, François. I am excited as well."

Montgomery listened to their conversation with curious intrigue. "Excuse me, a Grand Tour?"

Charlotte turned her attention back. "Why yes, whenever one of our esteemed pioneering ancestors returns to the planet after their long journey, we gather together to celebrate their greatness. Their accomplishments when they were most active on Earth."

Montgomery started to become excited as well. "This is wonderful!"

Charlotte smiled. "Then it's settled, we are all excited!"

"And François, you mentioned there was one a few years ago?" François nodded silently.

Charlotte interjected. "Yes, there was one a few years ago for Mr. Beckett, I believe."

"Beckett? You mean Winston Beckett?"

"Yes, that's correct."

"I adore Winston! He was a very close partner of mine. We did a lot of business together. I don't know how I would have kept my company afloat if it wasn't for his last-minute fuel deals. It kept us going until we could get more funding."

Charlotte continued smiling. "That's wonderful to hear."

"Yeah, do you know if he'll be there?"

Charlotte's smile sank slightly. "Oh no, I'm sorry Mr. Montgomery. Mr. Beckett passed away shortly after landing back to Earth."

"Oh." Montgomery went from excited to dejected. "That's... that's unfortunate. I would have loved to see him, especially now."

"Yes, we all felt his passing deeply." Her voice rose again. "But don't worry, Mr. Montgomery. You have a chance for a new life."

"That's good to hear. I want to see everything that has happened while I was away." He looked beyond the window in the carriage. "Does everyone ride in a carriage like this? Have we reverted back?"

François rolled his eyes, while Charlotte put her hand on his leg, helping him to not be so obvious with his disdain at the question. She looked at Montgomery.

"No, Mr. Montgomery. We bring the carriage to our special guests when they return. It is only for us and those like you." The carriage rolled over a bump, moving from the dusty trail to smooth pavement. "We are far beyond using carriages. See for yourself."

Montgomery poked his head out of the carriage door to see a world advanced beyond his dreams. There were platforms with trains speeding overhead, and people walking across large sidewalks and plazas talking to each other with three-dimensional displays floating in front of their faces. Colorful trees and flowers adorned the sleek cityscape, but the buildings were low enough to see a bright blue sky behind all of it. Cars drove past the carriage thoroughfare with melodies playing as each car passed over painted yellow markers. Montgomery peeked out and listened to the sweetest melodies flitting in the distance, oboes and violins and various hand drums.

"This is amazing."

"Yes, it certainly is. Our city is known for taking in refugees during conflict and is important in transportation and shipping." She stopped the explanation as Montgomery kept looking to see the fascinating sites of the city.

"And what is that sound coming from below?"

"The music? Our roads are built to charge the batteries for the drivers. The yellow patches in the road that you see are built in such a way that the friction of the road creates various pitches. When you string them together, you can make music. The city is full of these sounds, but they are most prominent in this area, which is why we call it the Euphony."

Montgomery saw how right she was. Storefronts played music over tiny speakers while the roads chimed away. So much to flood the senses, and yet everything fits together like a puzzle, all the pieces coming together to make a beautiful sonic mosaic.

"This is wonderful. I wish there was a way to capture this moment forever."

Charlotte and François turned to each other and smiled. Montgomery continued.

"You know, if he's still around, I was familiar with Derrick Winstead, the music mogul and famous producer. If he ever comes back, I think he'd love to get his hands on this place."

Charlotte and François turned to each other again, smiling less this time. François chimed in. "I believe I heard the name Winstead before. I think he landed somewhere else, Mr.

Montgomery. I believe his crash site was much further east."

Charlotte turned back. "Mr. Montgomery, this place truly is lovely. However, we must make haste on this trip. There are many things to see before the big celebration." She bowed her head slightly as she spoke in deference.

"Yes, that sounds good. I'm looking forward to what this place has to offer more and more." Montgomery was excited to see the celebration.

The carriage ride moved on to more specialized areas of the city. There were bread makers and storefronts where spices were being bagged and labeled. Soccer matches were taking place within fenced grass plots peppered across the special enclaves visible from the main street. Cars continued to glide by, and speedy trains darted to-and-fro against the backdrop of a setting sun. Families walked about, children tucked away in strollers or swaddled against their parents in colorful cloth wraps. Everyone wore flowy cotton cloth, scarves of gold and green, or tunics with silver and red trim. The streetlights flickered on, revealing coffeehouses and restaurants, hookah bars and singing lounges. The smell of chicken and lamb and vegetables, sweet cinnamon and peppery cardamom and earthy allspice, the roasted smells wafting through windows into every crevice of the city. Montgomery's senses lit up with enticement and inspiration.

The carriage came to a halt in front of a massive tent, adorned with lights and bursting with all sorts of scenes. Children were running around with sparklers. One ran past the horses, staring in wonder as to who might appear from such a carriage. The carriage driver hopped down from his seat and retrieved the stepstool for Montgomery, Charlotte, and François to alight. It was like all the city's sounds and smells had collected in this one place. Montgomery took a piece of kebab offered to him from one of many servers. François took several. Charlotte politely declined, and the server politely bowed.

"Mr. Montgomery, how have you felt about your return to our planet?"

"I am more impressed every moment. To think that so much has flourished in a part of the world that I would have never guessed would have such innovation."

Charlotte's face stiffened, but she maintained a smile. "That's quite... insightful."

Montgomery continued. "So, what is the occasion today?"

"It is a celebration of your return."

"Really?" Montgomery looked at a staging area in the center of the tent, illuminated by special lighting casting a purple disc above which a holographic image of his face floated. "How did you put this together so fast, and how did you know that I was coming back?"

"To answer your second question, our region monitors returns from the ancestral spacecraft. As I said before, there were some that have returned already. To answer your first question, we have developed a protocol for welcoming the ancestors back home. Signals were broadcast to everyone under our purview."

"What of the others not under your purview?"

"There have been others that have returned to other regions, and they have similar protocols. We keep a central database of those that have returned, as well as their ultimate fates."

"Fates? Are you saying that they didn't make it when they got back?"

"I am saying that they were not what we expected. Their time in space had changed them in some ways and not so much in others. Ultimately, they were not able to adjust to the changes." Charlotte paused for a moment. "All except one, that is."

Montgomery became increasingly giddy. "One person was able to manage. That means he could still be alive. Will I get a chance to meet him?." He hesitated to ask.

Charlotte smiled to herself slightly. "You assume it was a 'him'?" Montgomery felt embarrassed but was reassured. "Oh, I'm just teasing, Mr. Montgomery. I think you will have plenty of time. One way or another, we will be sure that you get a chance to meet *him*."

They leisurely made their way through the crowd. Montgomery and François continued taking food as waiters came by, while Charlotte continued to decline. While the two men reached their hands out constantly like crabs through the sand, Charlotte remained calm, graceful, and focused, as if gliding across the sea. She led them to a small area a few meters from the purple disc and hologram before she stopped and turned to Montgomery.

"Before we go in, we must give you something for the ceremony."

Montgomery was intrigued. "What exactly do you want to give me?"

Charlotte reached into a small hidden pocket in her dress. "Please stick out your tongue."

Montgomery stuck out his tongue without question while still trying to speak. "Wew, thith is unethpecthed."

She pulled out a tiny vial, unscrewed the top, and pulled out an even tinier eyedropper. "This is tradition for those that return. It opens your mind and allows you to see both the seen and the unseen. It is pleasure."

She carefully dropped a single drop onto Montgomery's tongue. Immediately he felt the liquid spread across his tongue, mouth, and lips.

"That was... unusual. Very noticeable. I wonder if it is like the drugs that we used to take."

Charlotte screwed the cap back on the tiny vial and secured it in her pocket. "I assure you—this is more potent than anything you can imagine. Come, let us take our place."

They moved into the circle. Charlotte directed Montgomery to sit on the ground, while she and François moved to either side of him. François pulled out his rod and—with the push of a single button—smoothly unsheathed it. He slammed it into the ground. The sound created a thunderous boom, silencing the crowd under the tent. Charlotte waited several moments until the voices hushed, then she addressed the crowd.

"Citizens of the Maghreb! We thank you for joining us in this new celebration. Another of our ancestors has returned to us from the far reaches. We honor those that paved the path to this moment." She extended her arm in Montgomery's direction. "See here—Mr. Herman Edward Montgomery the Third, a giant of industry in his time, a visionary in technology. For better or for worse, his actions brought us to this very moment, brought us together so that we could build a better future. Let us rejoice!"

All at once, people started ululating and holograms popped up across the crowd—displaying fireworks, a variety of festive creatures, and colors flashing back and forth. Meanwhile, actual fireworks shot into the sky, exploding into lights that cascaded against the night sky, just beyond the reaches of the tent. At this moment, the drug that Montgomery had been given started to take effect. Colors became more pronounced, and he saw spirits walking among the crowd. They resembled mannequins but were more lifelike, waving their arms and swaying between the holograms. They greeted each other as if they were old friends, reconnecting in the space of his mind after being separated in the ether. His eyes dilated. His smile widened. His breath opened. His mind was free.

After a few hours of celebration, eating and drinking and dancing and socializing, Montgomery stumbled towards Charlotte. "Charlotte, I have to say this is an amazing night."

"Thank you, Mr. Montgomery. We strive to give everyone the best possible experience."

"Truly wonderful. I would certainly love to meet the people that run this operation."

"Oh, why is that?"

"There are so many opportunities to do bigger things here." He pointed to a group of women hand-rolling individual pastries near the edge of the tent. "Can you imagine finding a way to make those ahead of time, packaged to sell? You could even keep them in a box somewhere for people to pick them up. That could really help with getting more of those delicious pastries to everyone." François approached while Montgomery spoke. "Oh, hello François, I was just telling Charlotte about all of the wonderful things we can do to improve this party."

François smiled at Charlotte. "Is that right?" He raised an eyebrow to acknowledge what he was hearing. "Please tell us what else we can do."

"Oh, so many things. For example, your performance earlier with the fireworks and the screams and all, was remarkable. But I did see that there were many people stationed around the tents to make sure that would happen. Now, if there was a way to connect them all, then maybe you would only need to have one person there. Then you could have others doing something else, or just more people at the party!" He started flailing his arms into the air, unsuccessfully attempting to keep up with the rhythm of the music playing.

"What wonderful ideas. We will be sure to bring them to the Welcoming Council when they meet next." François then turned to Charlotte. "*Sayidati, je demanderai au cocher de se préparer pour le voyage au mausolée.*"

"*Merci*, François." François excused himself as Charlotte turned back to her guest. "Mr. Montgomery, we have one final place for the Grand Tour, and we must make haste. The sun will be up in a few hours and we don't want to waste any time. You will need your rest."

"Ah, very well, Charlotte. While this party was in my honor, I think I may have overstayed my welcome. I'm looking forward to finishing the tour and getting back to work."

"Then there is not a moment to lose. Right this way." Charlotte led Montgomery away from the grounds and back to the carriage. The carriage driver had already placed the stepstool at the foot of the door for everyone to enter. François was already in the carriage when the others arrived.

"Driver, let us make haste," Charlotte commanded. "We must get to the final location soon."

"Yes, *Sayidati*."

Montgomery looked puzzled. "Hey, I forgot to ask. Your name is Charlotte, but others call you *Sayidati*. What does that mean?"

"*Sayidati* means 'madame'. It's a term of respect used to address those that are either of a higher status or those with whom you are unfamiliar."

"I see. You know, that's very interesting, Charlotte, because I once had to run a meeting in the South." He paused when he realized he was referring to the southern United States but did not even know whether it still existed. "Sorry, I meant the United States South. People there spoke like that a lot. Very formal. Not like where I'm from, so it was always a learning experience."

"That is very interesting, Mr. Montgomery. I'd like to hear more about it later." She stared out of the carriage.

Montgomery noticed that the sounds from the party dissipated quickly. "Hey, Charlotte, it sounds like the party died out all of a sudden. Is everything ok?"

"Oh yes, that is normal. This party lasted almost the entire night, and people need to rest."

"That makes sense." Montgomery started to yawn. "This might be a good time to start winding down."

"Please, not yet. This is as good a time as any. I was going to save your second dose of the special elixir that I gave you earlier." Charlotte once again reached into her pocket to retrieve the vial. "If you think one drop is potent, you should have another."

"Of course I'd like another. I felt so good after the first one." Meanwhile, the sounds from the party faded to silence, and the bright and colorful lights from the tents and fireworks suddenly disappeared into darkness. Montgomery stuck his head out of the window and looked back. "Hey, what happened? Did someone hit a light switch? Why did everything stop all of a sudden?"

Charlotte and François remained silent.

Several minutes later, the carriage appeared in front of a small building, illuminated by faint lights along the external walkway and the edges of the outer walls. In contrast to the rest of the city, this building was made of white marble and granite, strong yet plain-looking. It was not particularly tall, though it did have a modestly sized foyer. There were no adornments, no large, gilded structures, no bright colors nor artwork. Compared to what he saw previously, Montgomery was unimpressed.

"Well this is different. What is this place?"

Charlotte answered. "This is our final stop for our special guests that return. A place for us to record our tribute to you." The crew exited the carriage, and the driver descended and tied the horses to a nearby post. All four entered the building.

Montgomery was astounded by the silence. The building was rather small on the inside but echoed against smooth marble tiles and around thick Roman-style columns. There was no seating, only a large rock slab on the far end, across from the entrance. They could hear every movement when they proceeded to the rock slab.

Charlotte saw that Montgomery was curious. "Mr. Montgomery, we brought you here, as we brought all of those who returned to us. We understand this building is not as vibrant as the rest of our city, but it holds great importance to us. There are similar buildings like this in other parts of the world, to accommodate those that came back to us and landed in different places.”

“What is it?”

“It is a memorial to those who made sacrifices for us to reach here. We keep recordings, documents, other key pieces to remind us of where we came from, where we are, and where we hope to go in the future.”

When they walked closer, Montgomery started to see holographic images of people that he knew. Jonathan Baker, the coal and natural gas magnate. Susanna Herring, one of a long line of computer company chiefs. Edgemont Harris, the son of an Internet casino who spent his days flying from private island to private island, collecting money and women along the way. Philip Tennison, chief financial officer for the third largest fast food restaurant chain in the United States. And of course, Montgomery’s old friend, Winston Beckett.

“Hey, I know all these people. I remember meeting them at the orientation. Jon and Phil, I knew before that meeting.”

“Yes, Mr. Montgomery, we figured you knew them before, which is why it was so important for us to bring you here to be with them.”

Montgomery became emotional. He saw the dates of their deaths etched into the stone—they all had lived to more than one hundred and fifty years. "I'm glad the experiment worked and that they lived for so long. I hope their work affected you as mine did."

"Of course it did, Mr. Montgomery. You all had a role to play in how our society progressed." The driver produced a camera from a satchel that he brought into the memorial. "Our driver would like to take a picture of you as a memory of being here with us today."

"Certainly." Montgomery stood straight, his body angled, and his arms folded—a common pose for corporate photographs and marketing material. The pose came instinctively. The driver took several pictures in rapid succession.

"Thank you, Mr. Montgomery. We will make sure to use the best one. Or if one didn't come out well, we can accommodate some light editing."

"I'm sure it will be lovely. Thankfully, I won't have to worry about how it looks for a long while."

"Well, I wouldn't be so sure of that, Mr. Montgomery." She folded her hands together in front of her body, tilting her head slightly and smiling coyly. Behind Montgomery,

François used his rod as a crank to pry open a gap on the side of the rock slab, revealing another stone slab beneath. The slab slid out next to the holographic picture of Philip Tennison.

"What do you mean?" Montgomery asked just as the crank locked with a loud clank. The sound echoed against the walls. As the sound dissipated, Montgomery started to feel weak. His toes began to tingle, then the feeling started moving upwards, past his ankles, into his calves, then his thighs, and finally through the entire lower body. Without any feeling in his legs, he suddenly fell forward on his knees. His body jerked and he collapsed on his side.

"What? What's happening? I can't feel my legs. I can't feel my legs!"

Before Montgomery could say any more, François slapped a piece of thick tape across his mouth. Montgomery tried to fight him off, but he flailed his arms in vain as the numbness spread quickly to his hands. Suddenly his body felt like it was floating. François and the driver lifted him onto the slab that had appeared only a moment before, strapping his arms and legs down with leather restraints before he could find the will to escape. Charlotte began speaking as he protested through the tape.

"We don't have a lot of time, Herman, so it is best if you don't fight so hard." She shed all the formality. "I have to apologize for misleading you. While it's true that you are important, as were the others," she gestured her hand towards them, "it's not for the reasons you assume. When you all started the private space program many generations ago, our ancestors—our *true* ancestors—thought that this would bring a revolution to our whole civilization. That we would become the multiplanetary utopia that was promised to them for years and years. After promising them that our solutions on Earth would come from the stars. And so those in power sent you and your friends away in support of that project. And while your space pods zoomed through the universe, collecting data, and finding new places for humans to settle, the people here fought and starved. Droughts destroyed some places, floods engulfed others. The oceans rose and our hopes fell."

"My family had to flee the region that was once known as 'France'. We travelled south to the Maghreb, where the people treated my family better than anyone would have treated them in 'France'. And out of that kindness and compassion for others in need, we swore as a civilization that we would honor those that carried us through the worst. And so, we proceed as the children of survivors, who were made with sturdier stuff than we were. We still had the knowledge, so technology moved forward, but we also spent more time questioning whether we should pursue certain endeavors. Between the massive losses of life and the improvements to our way of life, we could survive for longer, without the pressure to propagate or advance our technology too quickly and to our detriment. Now, we do our best to manage human life—not with our advanced technology, which you have so kindly praised all day—but with our values, our norms, our morals. To put it in a way that you might understand, the solutions to our problems were never digital, they were always analog.”

She paced back and forth near the rock slab. “And even with all of that, with all of that suffering, we learned not to be bitter at those who abandoned us. But we knew that we had to do something if you and your kind ever returned.”

He was no longer receiving any preferential treatment as “Mr. Montgomery” by his hosts. He protested against the tape on his mouth. But with every word he struggled to scream, and with every labored breath through his nose, he could feel the numbness spreading into the rest of his body.

“Herman, you’re probably wondering about why you’re feeling this way.” She pulled out the vial from before. “You see, this liquid is potent. In fact, it’s why I carry so little of it, and why it comes with such a tiny dropper. One little drop acts as a very fun hallucinogen. It produces a euphoric state, heightening your senses so that you can get lost in the display you saw earlier. We give that experience to everyone who comes back. However, once we realize that the person hasn't changed, that they come back with the same mindset—to optimize endlessly, tinker with every process, every system, every institution—we know that they are hopeless. They bring back with them their desire to build skyscrapers and propulsion systems and space stations, to separate themselves from the rest of us. To be among the stars once more. To dance with the cosmos themselves. And yet, they can never be content to relax, enjoy a simple meal, and spend time with their fellow man without looking for new ways to exploit them. So we give them a second dose, which changes from a wonderful psychedelic to a wonderful… toxin." She spoke with a lilt in her voice, slightly giddy as the process unfolded.

"You will feel the toxin slowly creep through your body until it completely shuts down your body's ability to breathe or pump blood. That will take some time, maybe a full day or so."

Montgomery continued to scream through the tape, unable to move any other part of his body to escape. Both his will and his voice dampened with every attempt.

Charlotte grew bored with his muffled protests. She continued pacing back and forth, her delicate garments swishing through the dead air, the sliding of her slippers echoing across the floor like a rolling storm in the distance.

Meanwhile, François retrieved the rod from his pocket and pressed the button to extend its handle into a fully extended staff. Then, he pressed another button near the middle of the staff, which extended a spike and small axe blade from the top of the shaft. The entire contraption formed into a halberd, with finely sharpened edges that gleamed even under the low lights in the room. Rather than bring the halberd down to make a sound, he lifted it and balanced it on his shoulder, holding it with the blade side extending behind him.

Charlotte continued her speech. "Your efforts in your time may have been occasionally admirable. Not everyone has the gifts that you and I have. To orate. To inspire. To lead people to do things they may never have the courage or will to do on their own."

Montgomery's screams dampened further. The toxin's effect was deepening.

"But your resolve and inspiration should have been directed toward better things. Instead, you and people like you couldn't stop. You felt you never had enough. You could never stop taking. Every person was just another number, humans reduced to numbers, valued only in their performance of labor. Divorced from their humanity in the name of progress."

His vision was getting blurry. He lost feeling completely in his toes and fingers. His breathing was stable but slowing with each passing moment. Charlotte became more energized and more animated.

"There were so many of you so-called leaders. The least qualified of us to bring us to a truly equitable future. Casting people away from their vocations, their hard-earned jobs, to increase your profits every three months. Wrestling rights from people to grow food or collect rainwater on their own land. Antisocial sycophants managing the world's social interactions. Poisoning oceans, burning trees, war after war after unending war. And when the opportunity came to travel the universe, to turn our attention to the stars, sold as the way to find new solutions, it became a pet project for the wealthy to escape. To leave the rest to rot on Earth, for our ancestors' hopes and dreams to burn in endless fires and for their children to choke on the consequences of your bad decisions!"

She walked to the rock slab and smacked Montgomery across the face. His neck swung at the impact, his face nearly slamming into the rock. He whimpered while Charlotte composed herself.

"My apologies, Herman. I lost myself for a moment. I'm just... frustrated. You didn't even notice that one of you made it back and changed his ways."

Montgomery was confused. He lifted his head slightly to look around and see what she was talking about. Charlotte's outline loomed above him to his right, François just behind her. He looked straight between François' legs to see the driver.

The driver.

He squinted his eyes to better focus. He thought he could see the faded outline of...

Wait, it can't be...

The driver finally spoke again. "Did you finally figure it out, my friend?" He moved some of his garments from in front of his mouth. "It's me, Herman. Your old friend Garrett."

Charlotte interjected. "Yes, Herman. Garrett Johnson. I believe he was a hedge fund manager. Not the biggest company, but big enough to secure himself a seat on the ships."

Montgomery wanted to be more excited to see his friend. They had gone to business school together, completed the same internships, dated many of the same women, and stayed in touch while they grew their businesses. He loved Garrett and hoped that he would see him again. But something had changed about Garrett. Even in the increasing haze, he saw that Garrett was at peace. It was a far cry from his stress-filled days, his constant scheming and hustling for each contract and each dollar.

Garrett continued. "This place is wonderful, Herman. Being in space changed me. The vast emptiness of it all. I could feel it even in my stasis chamber. I saw just how small we were, how small we *are*, and how we needed to change. But when I came back, there really wasn't a place for my specific talents. They figured it out without us. Progress is still steady, but progress belongs to the people, not to us. So I was given the honor of driving the carriage during the Grand Tour. A fine way to see my old friends without being spotted so easily and convinced to go back to my old way of thinking. This place is fine as it is. We don't have to tinker with everything, to 'optimize' or 'reconfigure' or 'disrupt', or any of the many things we used to strive for. You could have lived in the moment. You could have lived freely."

Montgomery was crushed. This was not his friend. This was someone else, someone that no longer shared his values. Garrett was a better man. Montgomery had no more fight left in him. He accepted that this was where the tour stopped.

François brought the halberd down across Montgomery's leg, just under the knee. It landed with a loud bang. He felt nothing.

Charlotte closed her speech. "We are now preparing you for your final honors."

Another loud bang, this time cutting across Montgomery's other leg. Again, he felt nothing.

Garrett and François lifted his mutilated body onto an extending platform that came out of a wall opening. They placed Mongomery's severed legs upside down on each side of his head, creating a rectangular shape. He lay facing up, tears streaming down, looking at his feet and ankles beside his own face.

"Herman Montgomery, we thank you for your contributions to our society. Now, we ask that you please, kindly depart."

The platform slid into the opening, and the door closed. François stuck his halberd blade through a slot in the floor of the mausoleum, which cleaned, polished, and sharpened the blades back to a smooth finish. He pressed buttons on the halberd to retract its various parts for safekeeping. Garrett Johnson had cleaned his shoes, as well as the shoes of

Charlotte and François. He wanted to make sure no trace of Herman Montgomery left the mausoleum with them.

As a final act, François pressed a button above the small door to activate a three-dimensional holographic image of Herman Montgomery taken earlier in the day, smiling with a drink in hand and enjoying the party. Garrett Johnson led Charlotte Marroquin and François Khoury out of the mausoleum, where Charlotte and François each entered their own, separate black carriage and rode away to rest and conduct official business. Garrett mounted his carriage and went back to his own home, awaiting the next arrival.

Broken Persons

Jamie. One broken person.

Jamie's leg hurts again. Maybe a fracture. Maybe a strain. Maybe some chipped bone. Still hasn't gone to the doctor to find out one way or the other. Over two years since the pain started.

"It's fine, Sam. I think I'm managing it well."

That was a lie.

Taylor has been asking Jamie to join in soccer practice. Obviously, that can't happen with Jamie's injury, so I've been doing it. It's tough after a full week of work, especially knowing that Jamie signed Taylor up to be in club sports. Two practices a week after school, plus a game on the weekend. School ends before I'm scheduled to leave work, so I have to make up that time in my off-hours. What used to be my off-hours.

Whatever Jamie wants, I guess.

Jamie has started masking the pain. A lot of mild limping and leaning against furniture. Slightly better, but not great. I ask about going to physical therapy.

"No, I don't need to do that. I told you. I'm managing well."

We keep seeing commercials for medical services, ads for physical therapy, and social media posts about osteology services popping up in my feeds. Jamie keeps showing me the same ads. Every time.

"Isn't that weird? I'm not even talking about going. How would they know?"

I don't know. I think Jamie uses it as an opportunity to assert that medical assistance is off the table.

Taylor's team made it to the playoffs. I have a work event today. It would be a good opportunity for me to get some face time and maybe even advance in my career. But Jamie's leg is especially sore today, and Jamie can't drive.

I'm doing my best to get some work done on my phone from the bleachers. Reviewing my team's reports. Approving timesheets. Conducting research on laws and regulations. More reports. Accepting a chance to lead a new initiative. Doesn't pay more, but it moves me a bit closer to getting that big promotion. More reports, with a few that need direct comments.

Suddenly, massive cheering breaks out in the bleachers. My attention diverts away from the phone. Taylor scored the game-winning goal. Ninety-third minute of the game. People from both sidelines are shouting, Taylor's team in joy, the opposing team in anguish. I don't even know where the other team is from. I don't even really know anyone from our side. Taylor is looking at me to see how happy I am. I feign a smile as if I had been watching the whole time. I wasn't. Taylor notices.

We're finally back in the car, heading home. "Did you see me score that last one?"

"Of course, I did! It was such a great goal."

"What did you like about it?"

"That you helped the team win!"

Taylor sounds skeptical. "What about the other goal I made?"

Another goal? I have to make up something.

"Oh yeah, that one was great, too. You couldn't have won without the other one as well."

Taylor slumps deeper into the seat.

"What's wrong?"

"I didn't score any other goals."

The rest of the drive home passes in silence.

Taylor goes straight upstairs. Shower and a nap, the normal routine. Jamie is nowhere to be found. I can hear glasses clanking from the basement. Jamie's at the downstairs bar, drinking again. Anything to take the pain away. Anything but a doctor's visit. Anything but therapy.

I walk to the kitchen to prepare dinner. Taylor comes down a few hours later, rested and probably finished a bit of schoolwork. Taylor is great. We're eating baked chicken and fettucine alfredo with minimal conversation. Talk about school and expectations for the next week with soccer. Planning out a schedule. Surface-level things tonight, nothing deep. Taylor cleans the dishes while I sweep the floors and clean the countertops. Taylor retires, more reading and maybe playing some video games.

Jamie never comes upstairs. I open the door to the basement to hear faint snoring. Asleep again. Also, part of the normal routine.

Whatever Jamie wants, I guess.

I can hear Jamie waking up in a mood. At least the whole night wasn't spent in the basement. I leave breakfast on the table before Taylor and I go grocery shopping. Tomatoes, beans, protein bars, a couple heads of lettuce, some baby spinach. Check. I get myself a chocolate chip cookie and a sugar cookie for Taylor as a bonus treat. Also, to get back in good graces for yesterday's game. We talk about what happened. How I am sorry for not being present to watch each moment, how I wish I wasn't so tired all the time and how I want to be there, not just with my body but also with my attention. Taylor knows it's been tough, and that I need space to focus on work to help support the family. Taylor's a good kid. Time to get home.

The house is a mess. We haven't been gone that long. I can hear Jamie struggling across the floor, lugging that busted leg.

"Is that you Sam? Can you bring me something to eat?"

The breakfast I left is still on the table. Taylor starts putting the groceries in the fridge while I take the plate of food and a fork upstairs. Jamie is just sitting on the edge of the bed, looking at memes online.

"Thanks, Sam. I appreciate it. You made this fast."

"You're welcome. Why didn't you just eat it when you were downstairs?"

Jamie looks confused. "I didn't see any plate down there."

"But it was right on the table. You had to have passed it to get to whatever you were doing."

Jamie drops the fork on the plate, still chewing a mouthful of food. "Come on, Sam. Do you really have to do this? I told you I didn't see it. Please stop bothering me."

I'm too stunned to say anything. I could just start yelling, screaming about all the neglect and oversight of basic things in the house, but that would cause a fight. And Jamie would completely shut down and I wouldn't be able to get anything done for days. I have a busy workweek coming up. The busiest. I have to bite my tongue and hope for some clarity and peace.

"Sure thing." I turn and walk out of the room without much fanfare.

Taylor has already put away the groceries and is sitting on the couch searching for movies to watch on television.

"Hey Tay, I'm going to work for a bit."

"...okay, love you!"

I go to the basement. The stench of stale alcohol is wafting in the air and the old couch is stained. No worries. I just lay down and sob quietly.

Whatever Jamie wants, I guess.

Jamie is nowhere to be found. Not able to do any work around the house, lest it aggravate the leg, but still able to leave the house for whatever reason. I reach into the fireplace to open the flue. I have to clean the fireplace out before winter comes. I don't pay attention. The flue door slams right on my arm after I had just finished cleaning the thing. The drive to the hospital isn't so bad. The wait is longer than usual, but my issue is routine. Priority is given to more serious issues. Potentially losing a limb, heavy bleeding, that sort of thing. There is even a gunshot victim that has to be rushed in. Nurses say it looks like a full recovery but needs to be sure. In any case, it delays the help that I need.

Triage. Consult. X-rays. Images are no good. More X-rays. More waiting. Finally, I see the doctor. Nothing broken but seriously aggravated. This will need some physical therapy. I'm skeptical.

"Well Sam, whenever you're ready, I can provide you a referral."

"Thank you, doctor."

I try to avoid discussion of physical therapy. Jamie will think I'm suggesting it for the leg. That's the thinking, as if everything I feel or do must center around Jamie's needs. I keep my mouth shut about everything. No need to worry. No need for static. No need for drama. I make dinner through the pain. Taco bowls. Not bad, actually.

Jamie keeps asking me for things. A pillow to raise the leg, a towel to dry some spilled tea near the living room couch, some peanuts and chocolate chips for dessert, some more peanuts for an after-dessert snack.

"Jamie, I can't keep bringing these things, I hurt my arm today."

"Hurt your arm? Doing what?"

"I was cleaning the flue."

"Sam, I told you I was going to get a guy to do that later this week."

"Yes, but you've been saying it every week for the last month."

Jamie sighs. "Here we go again, bothering me about things."

I roll my eyes and walk away in a huff. "Never mind. I won't bother you with this."

Jamie realizes it's gone too far and leans up from the couch. "Sam, please don't go."

"Look, I'm sorry for thinking you would do something about it. I don't need anything from you. I've got it."

"Okay, look, I'm sorry about not calling sooner." I turn around. I'm not sure why. In these moments, I somehow hope that Jamie is actually listening and will choose to take steps to get help. "Look, I'll be more mindful next time. I think I just need to set a reminder for myself. But please stay so we can all watch together."

I sit next to Jamie on the couch, that busted leg perched across my lap. Just then I realized that our child had been sitting on the floor the whole time, listening to this argument. I lean forward a bit to see Taylor's face. It's blank, eyes looking forward at the screen and avoiding paying attention to us. Taylor has heard this fight before and would rather not deal with it tonight.

So here we are, Jamie and Sam. Two broken persons.

Whatever Jamie wants, I guess.

———————————————————————————

It's been over a week, and the pain is starting to radiate through my arm and extend to my shoulder. I've been trying to keep it together to keep the peace with Jamie, but I can't take it anymore. I call my doctor about that referral for physical therapy, then I call to make an appointment. Thursday, six o'clock in the evening. Just after work. It'll take about twenty minutes to get there, so I'll need to be quick about it.

I tell my family about it. Taylor is upset that I will miss a rare Thursday night soccer game but understands what I need to do to recover. Jamie accuses me of casting shame about the injury. That I am trying to push an agenda to rehab the busted leg. I don't care about that leg. I don't care about any of what Jamie is trying to do. I just want to heal myself.

It's finally Thursday, and I can start the process of recovery. Driving is difficult with only one arm, but I manage. Still, having to drive like this is making my hand hurt really badly.

The doctor's staff at the therapy clinic is nice, and the facility is simple, yet clean. Doris, the receptionist, walks me to a seat attached to a small contraption where I can rest my sore arm and weary, throbbing hand. Dr. Halpert takes a look and asks me about my life while randomly pressing in between the tendons and bones. I talk about work, about Taylor, about someday visiting Prague and Vienna. She nods and talks about her three kids and her most recent vacation to Bermuda.

She says that the original diagnosis was correct. Nothing is broken. There is trauma near the wrist and forearm, and the other pain is a result of overcompensating to stabilize the injury. That's alright for a few days, she says, but eventually it will wear down strength in my hand, wrist, and forearm, and it could lead to a far worse situation in the future. Therapy will probably take about six months for full recovery.

Taylor makes dinner for the family while Jamie lays on the couch in a crabby mood. Taylor's a good kid. Jamie complains about me going to therapy, then asks for tips on how to help with a busted leg.

"Jamie, it's an arm, not a leg."

"Yeah, but I figured I could get some tips from you."

"I don't think that's how it works."

Jamie is frustrated but flashes an awkward smile. "...okay, whatever you say."

I'm not concerned anymore with the attitude. I give Taylor a kiss on the cheek and ask to have my food packed for lunch tomorrow. I'm not hungry, and Taylor understands. Taylor is a good kid.

I go to sleep, the discomfort in my arm slightly relieved, looking forward to my next steps toward healing.

It's been two weeks and my therapy has been going well. There is still some weakness, but I'm able to do more with my arm. I've been doing a lot of rotation, gripping exercises, and some light lifting. I've been able to sit at a computer and work more. I've been able to help Taylor practice soccer in my spare time, now that I don't wince every time I move. I'm in a better mood.

Jamie has been watching me over these last couple of weeks. Being happy. I can see some contempt in Jamie's eyes, but also a bit of longing.

"Sam, I think I'd like to consider going to therapy for this leg."

I am taken aback. "Really?"

"Yeah, I think it's time."

I never thought this day would come. "Okay. Well, would you like me to help get some referrals? I think my company has some programs."

"Yes, please. I'll look at some things as well."

This is great. Jamie is finally willing to get some help, to start healing, and hopefully take some of the physical load off me.

Now that Taylor is asleep, I open my laptop computer and start pulling up listings for doctors that take our insurance plan. There is a good general practitioner not too far from where we live, and there are several well-reviewed orthopedic surgeons not too far either. We can get more guidance once Jamie decides to see the doctor and figures out a plan.

Things are looking up.

It's been almost two weeks, and I haven't heard anything from Jamie about finding a good doctor.

"Jamie, have you heard anything from any of the doctors that you reached out to?"

"No, I called a couple of them and haven't heard anything. I think I'm just not going to do it."

"You called how many?"

"A couple."

"And no one responded?"

"Nope."

"It might be because of all the pandemic stuff. A lot of the offices haven't gotten back to full capacity."

"Maybe. I don't think I'm going to do it."

I'm confused. Surely someone would have called back. "What about the ones I emailed to you?"

Jamie looks up at me with a crooked face. "Oh, those? I didn't even bother reaching out to those names."

I'm doing my best to contain my rage. I know that if I start to scream, Jamie will shut down and disappear into the bedroom for the rest of the day. "Hmm... ...okay." I nod, then I go back to the couch to read articles on my phone. I think I've had enough of Jamie for today. I'm going to focus on helping Taylor and finishing some housework. I realize that I can't count on Jamie to fix that busted leg. I'll need to make sure I have enough strength to deal with physical labor in the house moving forward.

Whatever Jamie wants, I guess.

Jamie's friends from college emailed today. They want to get everyone together to do some activities they haven't done in a long time. Pickup soccer games, indoor rock climbing, hiking around the lake. Jamie was trying to rationalize participating.

"It should be fine. I'll be fine. Everything will be okay. If I go, I should be able to some of the things, right?"

I politely nod.

"I mean, it's not going to be dangerous. I know I've been in some pain, but it should be fine."

I politely nod again.

"Yeah, it should be fine. I don't need to worry about my leg."

Once again, I nod.

"Why aren't you saying anything? You listening to me?"

I turn my head nonchalantly. "Yes, love. I hear you. You can do whatever you want." I take my book and my computer and walk upstairs to our room.

Later that night, Jamie walks into the room while I'm reading.

"Sam, I just realized something. I need to be serious about going to physical therapy."

I look at Jamie blankly, waiting to hear more of the explanation.

"It's like, I started rationalizing how I was going to be okay. And I never had to do that. I would just... *do* things. And once it started going through my head, I realized that I should do something about it."

I can't muster any enthusiasm; my voice is reserved and monotone. "Very good, Jamie. Let me know if there is anything I can do to help."

Jamie feels good about the decision and hops into bed. I place my book on the nightstand and roll over. The light goes out and I feel Jamie's arm around my waist. It would seem that I'm little spoon tonight. Jamie might get frisky later. I'm unimpressed.

Two months of physical therapy. Well, two months for Jamie, longer for me. We're starting to see real results. The busted leg is not so busted right now, and even though there might be some nagging damage later, Jamie has been more active and less depressed. With all that healing, I haven't had to be around to do as much of the physical work, which has given me time to pursue other things—cleaning more around the house, taking walks around the neighborhood for extended periods, helping Taylor practice soccer more. And my mental load is better, because I can focus so much more on office obligations, I don't have to work until crazy hours catching up on unfinished tasks. Even our sex life... I've been *in the mood* more. Things have really moved in the right direction.

"Hey Sam, I'm going to quit physical therapy. Is that cool?"

I am confused. Jamie just walks down the stairs and blurts this out.

"What do you mean?"

"Well, I've been going for a couple of months, and I'm not feeling any different, so I'm just going to stop going."

Everything starts to bubble up again. *How can Jamie do this?* The doctor said it was going to take a few more months because of the damage from not taking care of it sooner. *How can you not feel any differently? What about all that progress?* All that work is going to go down the drain. I know what's going to happen now. That leg is going to get busted again, and we're going to slowly come back to all the habits from before. The dull pain. Me having to take over so much physical load. Driving Taylor everywhere, all by myself. I see it coming for me. I don't have the patience anymore. I don't even have the mental strength to ask.

"That's fine, Jamie. Whatever you want to do."

"Yeah, I think I'm healed enough. I'll let them know that I'm not coming." Jamie casually walks back upstairs.

If you say that you're healed, how do you not feel any different?

The contradictions don't matter. Not to Jamie. And certainly not to me anymore.

Whatever Jamie wants, I guess.

It's been three weeks, and I'm already seeing signs of things reverting to what they were. First, Jamie can't take out the trash because of a weird sensation in the big toe. Then, we can't go to a friend's party because they have a steep driveway and Jamie's ankle is sore. Don't want our friends to see what's going on, I guess. Taylor has a big game, but Jamie's depressed from the pain. Well, not "depressed," because Jamie doesn't call it "depressed."

"I'm feeling a little down. Not sure why. Anyway, I can't go to the game."

Jamie stops paying attention to what I'm saying. Just asks me about things and then zones out to a television screen or a phone. It's frustrating, to say the least, but it doesn't matter. I'm spiteful now. I stopped going to physical therapy as well. Four more sessions before I'm officially cleared, but I don't see the point. *Why should I spend my time trying to heal just to compensate for someone else?* Let my arm start to hurt.

Jamie can't walk to the kitchen to pour coffee? Sorry, I can't pour with my messed-up arm.

Can't walk the trash to the curb? How am I supposed to carry the can?

Cleaning? Can't do that. Cooking? Might as well order in. Sure, it costs more, but that's what we're doing here.

It's what you want, Jamie. It's *whatever. You. Want.*

Life is hard for Taylor. Jamie is stubborn, and I don't communicate. These are our problems. On the other hand, Taylor realizes that life can't go on this way. Taylor does the cooking. And the cleaning. And tending to all the house's needs. Jamie and I still work, but everything else has fallen on our child. Taylor was making it work for a while, but there are just too many demands, so no more soccer. No extracurricular activities outside the house and not much time to read, other than what is required for school. No time to go out with friends, in case either Jamie or I end up in a serious accident. No gaming because that's too distracting and we need Taylor alert. Just last week, Jamie tried to leave after a shower and slipped on the edge of the bathtub trying to get out. Slammed into the wall. No blood, but still scary. Jamie couldn't see straight for about fifteen minutes. I bumped into the edge of a doorway and felt like my arm was going to fall off.

Taylor walks through the front door as Jamie and I sit on the couch watching trashy reality television. "Hi everyone." Jamie doesn't say anything.

"Hello, Taylor. Do you have schoolwork today?"

"No, I made sure to do everything during class today. Didn't want to get in the way of stuff I need to do around here." I can hear shoes coming off and a backpack falling to the floor, filled with books and loose papers.

"How are you feeling Taylor?"

"Meh."

"Do you want to sit with us and watch TV?"

Taylor walks to the sofa chair silently and settles in, laying horizontally across the chair, plopping both feet over the armrest. We don't say a word to each other. We don't say much at all.

So here we are. Jamie, Sam, and Taylor. Three broken persons.

Whatever I want, I guess.

A Nice Lunch

"You found a job?"

Helen sat on the patio at a long table directly across from Matthew. She was dressed in a long, flowing, white cotton dress with an ornate trim. She wore a matching cotton head wrap and some light sandals. Matthew wore gray sweatpants and a white T-shirt, caked with various colors of paint, and blue skateboarding shoes. His hands had paint marks, even under his fingernails, and a few drops of dried paint stretched and cracked across his face and neck as he ate.

"I've always had a job, Mom."

"Matthew, be serious. Painting is not a job."

"I don't just paint, Mom. You know that. I have steady work." He reached over the table for the broccoli and scooped it onto his plate.

"Well, when your sister gets here, you should ask her about getting a better job." She delicately placed another bite of food into her mouth with her hands.

Dej, Matthew's father, was sitting next to his mother. He wore brown corduroy pants with a green long-sleeved shirt. As always with his top two buttons were unbuttoned. He silently gnawed at a portion of roasted short ribs.

Matthew kept his head down trying to minimize the conversation. "Whatever."

"I'm serious. You know, you're so smart. You should have been a lawyer. I expected Samia to be a doctor, and you would be a lawyer. But I'm fine with her becoming a lawyer. I just wish that you weren't so lazy."

Matthew slammed both hands down onto the table, then slowly raised his eyes toward his mother.

"I'm so tired of you saying that."

Helen looked back at him with unwavering eyes. She was unsurprised by how he was acting. "Look, just relax, okay? We're just having a conversation."

Matthew raised his voice slightly. "Why do we have this same conversation every time I come here? Can we just have a peaceful meal for once?"

Unbothered, Helen continued with her meal, shrugging her shoulders, and grabbing up another morsel of chickpea stew and steamed baby carrots. "Whatever you say. You could just be nice, though."

Matthew let out a deep sigh, then picked up a few broccoli florets and shoved them in his mouth. The only sounds during lunch were those of dishes sliding across the table and their chewing.

After a few minutes, Samia appeared, walking through the fence gate, holding a bag labeled "Ted's Bakery."

Helen was elated. "Hey, Samia! It's good to see you." She stood up from the table to greet and give Samia a big hug, which let everyone know that she was excited to see her. In Mom's house, you were not permitted to get up from the table until the meal was done. Unless you were Mom. Mom could break the rules. The rest could not.

"Hello, hello." Samia greeted everyone with a hello and a nod. Dad silently raised his hand and nodded. Matthew chimed back, "Hey, Samia. What's up?"

"Oh, nothing much. Just bringing some dessert."

Helen was grinning from ear to ear. "You didn't have to bring anything. We're just happy to see you." Matthew scrunched his face as he suspiciously looked at his mother. She had been complaining a few minutes before Samia came, about how he always came to the house empty-handed, even though he neither had a lot of money to spend on treats and nor extra time to make anything. Helen knew that.

Helen always said something anyway. "Are you staying for lunch?"

"I can't stay for too long. I have to get back to work."

Helen led Samia to the empty seat between Dej and Matthew. "Oh, that's unfortunate. But it's Sunday, you should be resting."

Samia folded her flowing floral dress to sit in the chair. Helen went back to her seat at the makeshift head of the table.

"I can take a little food. Thank you, Mom." She patted her father on the leg affectionately, then turned to her brother. "Hey, how's your painting going?"

"Eh, it's okay."

Their mother butted in. "I keep telling him that he needs to do something else with his time. It's a hard life. I should know, I used to be an artist."

Matthew spoke up, calm but audibly exasperated, while Samia put her head in her hands. She knew a fight was going to start. Dej continued cutting his meat and eating. "Mom, you were not an artist. You took two art classes."

"Matthew, don't say that. That is very rude." She tried to keep herself calm but could not hide her sneering. She looked like she was going explode at any moment if he continued talking to her that way.

Matthew looked down at his cup of black coffee and continued. "It's true. Tell me where any of your art is. I haven't seen it."

"Matthew!" Her face started to feel warm, and she clenched her hands into fists.

Samia interjected while gesturing with her hands. "Okay, okay, can we please talk about something else? I don't want another meal to be *this* thing again." Matthew daintily sipped his coffee. Helen let the tension in her body loosen, then carefully collected a small bite of food in her hand. Dej dipped a piece of meat into a mixture of dry spices and ate it, chasing it with a sip of beer. It did not take long before Samia broke the silence.

"I had a good evaluation at work. I might be up for a promotion next year."

"That's so great!" Helen continued her praises. "It's really wonderful to see how much you have accomplished at work." She then raised her voice slightly, just enough to emphasize her next point to the rest of the table. "Look what you accomplish when you *really* focus and go into a career path with a lot of potential."

Matthew understood the subtext. *You are wasting your life.* It was more of the same, and he had had enough of that particular conversation. He softly took his napkin from his lap and placed it on the table as he stood. "I'm going to take a walk."

Despite Helen's words, she did not want him to leave. "No, son, please stay at the table."

Samia agreed. "Yeah, Matthew, please stay with us. Let's finish lunch together."

"No, thank you. I've had plenty."

His sister tried to keep him close. "Here, let's walk together."

"No, Samia, you can stay with Mom and Dad."

"It's okay, I just got here. I can eat later. Come with me." She grabbed his hand and stood with him. He casually protested but allowed her to come along. They walked through the patio door and through the house. Helen and Dej stayed at the table as she asked, "What did I do?" Dej shook his head and continued eating meat.

Meanwhile, Samia and Matthew walked through the front door and sat on the porch stairs. Samia took out a pack of cigarettes and a lighter. "You want one?"

Matthew shook his head. "No thanks. I'm trying to chill with that."

"Okay, no problem." Samia lit her cigarette and took a drag, holding it between her index and middle fingers.

"You know Mom is probably going to smell that."

"It's fine, she loves me." Samia smiled and winked at Matthew while she said it. She knew she was the favorite just as well as he did, and she sometimes ribbed him about it.

"Ha, I know."

"Seriously, man, how are you?"

"Not bad, actually. Money is a little tight, but I just signed a big contract for some murals and some graphic design work. Just waiting for my advance to clear on both of them."

"That's great! That's a big deal."

"Thanks."

"Did you tell Mom and Dad? Maybe they'll get off your back about money." She took another drag.

"I already told them. They don't listen to me. They think that I'm just getting a little bit of money and that it's not secure, even though most of what I'm doing now is government work."

"You need to find a way to explain it better. Get them to listen."

"How do you tell someone who doesn't listen that they don't listen?"

Samia took another drag and thought about what her brother had just said. "You know, you make a good point."

"Exactly. That's why I just let her think whatever she wants to think and keep doing what I'm doing."

"Has Dad said anything to her?"

"Is Dad allowed to say anything?" Samia nodded silently in agreement before Matthew continued. "So, what did you do this weekend? You're usually caught up with work by Saturday."

"Usually, but we're working on a really tough case. I knew I was going to work on Sunday anyway, so I went out with some friends."

"Where did you go?"

"Tavern Zee."

"And who did you make out with?"

Samia laughed. "Ha! Who *didn't* I make out with?"

Matthew chuckled. "Do you think Mom would approve of such behavior?"

"See, that's where your problem is. You're *too* honest with Mom."

"It's too much stress for me to not do that."

"It's already stressful when you're so forward. You have to tell her the truth that *she* wants."

"I know, but it's tough for me."

"See what I did before out there?" She pointed in the direction of the backyard with her cigarette hand. "Staying for a little bit to work later today? That's the truth. She knows not to ask me about anything else. Give her something that she can brag to her friends about, and she'll leave you alone."

"I'll do what I can. I can't help it sometimes." He reached his hand out to Samia, signaling for the cigarette pack. She opened the pack and pointed it in his direction. He slid a cigarette out and lit it with Samia's lighter. He took a drag while she put out her first cigarette and lit a second.

While they continued talking on the porch, they heard their father walk through the house and upstairs with his signature heavy gait. He had left the table to use the restroom next to the master bedroom. He saw his children on the porch but did not say anything to them as he walked by. As he sat on the toilet, he pulled out his phone to read through some articles— global politics, business and finance, or just general drama regarding figures in public life. He calmly sat, occasionally chuckling or mildly shocked over something extreme, like a near-coup attempt in a remote part of the world or a new scientific discovery.

Helen was not patient, especially with everyone away from the lunch table.

After adjusting her headwrap, she stood up from the table and walked back into the house with the empty pitcher. After removing her shoes at the patio door, she walked into the kitchen and filled it at the faucet. Then she took out the ice tray from the freezer and carefully dumped all twelve ice cubes into the pitcher. She set the pitcher on the island in the center of the kitchen and walked upstairs.

Dej finished on the toilet but sat there for a while, continuing to flip through his feed. While skimming an article on civil strife in Eastern Europe, a pop-up with a buxom, conventionally attractive woman appeared on his phone. Unfortunately, it also appeared when Helen opened the bathroom door and barged in.

"What are you looking at?" She snatched the phone from his hand and looked at the image.

From downstairs, Samia and Matthew heard a loud crash coming from the master bedroom. They looked at each other in surprise to confirm what they both had just heard.

"I'll go see what's going on." Matthew stood up to walk in and stepped on his nearly spent cigarette. He opened the front door and walked upstairs, only to find his father on top of his mother, pinning her to the bed with one arm while lifting his slipper with his free hand above her as if ready to strike. She was screaming incoherently at him, holding a lamp. He stayed silent.

"What are you doing?!?" Matthew darted in and grabbed his father's hand, freeing his grip from the slipper. He pulled his father away, allowing his mother to spring up from the bed.

"*Shermuta!*" Helen screamed in anger, pointing at Dej. "I told you I would catch you!" She then pointed at Matthew. "Look at this!" She shoved the phone in front of Matthew to provide the "evidence." Dej simply sucked his teeth and walked away. Helen continued, breathing heavily. "You see how he attacked me.

"Mom, this is just a pop-up ad."

"It's an ad for prostitutes... look!"

Sure enough, it was an advertisement for male enhancement pills. "Mom, this is just a pop-up. I don't think dad was... "

She snatched the phone back. "I shouldn't tell you these things. You never listened to me. I should have shown Samia. Daughters are better at listening to their mothers anyway, not like sons. Not like you." She sat down on the bed whimpering.

This hurt Matthew, but it was an expected response. His mother had been saying things like that for years, any time he or his father did something of which she did not approve. Never about Samia though, only them. It did not matter to him at that moment. His father was about to hit his mother.

Matthew sat next to his mother on the bed, tentatively rubbing her back to make her feel better. He was not used to seeing his mother show any vulnerability in front of him. He rubbed the top of her back in a slow, circular motion, which helped her relax. She did not look up from her husband's phone, which had gone into locked mode. She sniffled and attempted to choke back her sobbing. There were no tears, only a small glimmer in her eye that refused to budge. The lamp that she used to defend herself was on the bed to her right, the paper-thin lampshade torn and the base scratched.

Matthew slid off the bed and looked around the room to see if there was any damage to anything else. He did not see any broken glass or shards on the furniture or in the carpet. He saw some streaks in the carpet indicating that someone walked through it, and he saw that some of the jewelry on his mother's dresser had shifted. *This fight must have gone all over the place*, he thought. Fortunately, he did not see any other damage, so he sat back on the bed by his mother's left side. He sat with his hands folded, looking around the room awkwardly. Soon, his gaze moved to his left, where he saw his father's dresser—his wallet, some old business cards, forty dollars in cash, and his watch, all sitting under his father's lamp.

Wait... his father's lamp.

He looked back at the lamp next to his mother, then he looked behind him to check his mother's dresser again. Jewelry, keys, some makeup from earlier... and no lamp.

"Mom," he asked. "What happened in here?"

"Look, Matthew, I don't want to talk about it."

"Yeah, I understand. But I just wanted to ask. Did Dad attack you?"

"Yes, son. I grabbed his phone, and as soon as I took it, he tried to hit me."

"Okay. And you grabbed the lamp to defend yourself?"

"Yes, I didn't want him to hit me, so I had to grab the lamp first."

Matthew took a deep breath and closed his eyes. "Okay, Mom, remember that I love you. I'm going to ask this, and I don't want you to get upset." Helen looked up at her son as he took another breath. "If he attacked you right after you took the phone, then why did you take your own lamp?"

Helen was confused. "I don't understand."

"So, you took the phone, then he immediately attacked you."

"Yes. What are you saying?"

"Then, I would think that you would grab the lamp from his dresser. Why do you have the one from your dresser?"

Helen started looking around the room, up and down, left, and right. Anywhere except at her son. "I ran back there to get the lamp so that I could protect myself."

"Okay, so did he come after you? Or did he wait here?"

Helen now looked back at her son defensively. "Matthew, what are you trying to say?"

"I'm trying to figure out what happened, because if we need to call the police, then---"

"No! We're not going to call the police. Just leave it alone."

"Mom, if he attacked you, then he can't get away with that. But if something else happened, then we need to know."

"I said no!" Helen went silent. She was not going to tell Matthew what happened. She was not going to admit that she was wrong about the picture on his phone, and she was not going to admit to attacking him first.

Matthew looked at her, shook his head, and walked out the door. Helen sat stoically for a moment, then went into the bathroom to fix her headwrap and makeup. Matthew walked back to the patio, and Samia was waiting for him at the base of the steps.

"What happened up there?"

Matthew was stone-faced as he walked past her. "Don't worry. Maybe I'll tell you about it later."

Dej was already sitting at the table, finishing the last of his meal. Matthew sat down and chugged a glass of water. Samia sat at her position, confused as to what was happening. She took a few strawberries and a banana and ate silently.

Helen returned to the table a few minutes later, clothing and hair in perfect order. She sat in her seat and continued drinking her coffee, which had since cooled. They sat for several minutes in silence, not looking up from their respective plates.

Samia finally broke the tension. "So, I have a really long day tomorrow and need to get ready. I think I should go." No one responded. "Matthew, I'm heading your way, so I can drop you off if you want."

"That would be great, thanks." Matthew stood up from the table along with Samia. "Mom, Dad, it's always a pleasure. Never change."

Samia and Matthew walked toward the back gate and left.

Helen was agitated about the entire affair. She picked up a loaf of bread, tearing handfuls from the loaf and eating them voraciously. Dej finished off his meat and sipped his coffee. He sarcastically said the only thing that came to mind as Helen glared.

"That was a nice lunch."

Last Message for the Wanderer

His name escaped him.

The Wanderer had travelled for several years, shuffling through sand and bone, stumbling over the remains of human civilization. Cars, metal signs, frayed electrical wires, various trinkets and gadgets buried under nature's wrath. The world continued to disappear under his feet with each day.

He was weary, and voices echoed in his head relentlessly. He could never figure out the source of those voices.

Are these voices coming from long-forgotten frequencies?

Are there still some malfunctioning devices near the surface? Were they just that prolific?

How many children's toys once responded to tiny voices and now respond to the high pitches of harsh winds and birds of prey?

Are these voices just in my head after so many months of solitude?

He was so lonely.

The memory of his name was the last to leave him. Before that, he was a "project management specialist," whatever that meant. The truth was that he was a generic paper-pusher, badgering recent college graduates to deliver spreadsheets and pretty charts from one overpaid middle manager to another slightly-less overpaid middle manager, making sure that the right colors and shapes were telling other overpaid people with fancier job titles how to make decisions so that a little line could trend up every three months. That little line was the only thing important to the investors. It did not matter what they created, or what harm they caused. It only mattered that the line went up every three months so that no one lost their jobs. And even then, people still lost their jobs to make sure the line went up. Those people would go to other places where they did the same thing, until they could become the new overpaid middle managers, forcing a new group of twenty-somethings to do the same thing.

Before he became a Wanderer, he convinced himself that this was the right way, enough to make a nice living for himself and his family. He could take his family out for a nice dinner each Friday night, a movie or play each Saturday, have enough money to tithe on Sunday, and enjoy a comfortable two-week vacation each year. Occasionally, he could take a day of golfing or a night out for beers with his friends, maybe some flirtation with a waitress or two. Nothing serious, just something to make him feel special, like he still had some youth and vigor. This went on for eight years, and despite his otherwise bland personality, the people in his life seemed to enjoy his company.

None of that mattered anymore. It did not matter because there were no more places left to vacation, nor any golf courses or bars. It did not matter because there were no more churches or places to work. It did not matter when there was no longer a family for which to care.

The Wanderer stubbed his toe and tripped face-first into the sand. He quickly got up, wiping away the sand from his face and out of his mouth and nose. He looked down to see what he had tripped on—a metal sign. He hurriedly dug through the sand to unearth the sign, trying to make sense of where he was. He had walked for what felt like hours, but his sense of time was off. He pulled back the shirt that he had wrapped around his head and tucked back the tie he was using as a belt. The reflective green sign came into focus, and a white "S" appeared. It was perfect—a metal exit sign for a major road. He dug faster, pulling on the sign as he pushed handfuls of sand away from it. Soon, the sign was free.

Springfield. He was not too far from where he grew up. But where exactly was he?

He knew that the sun had been setting for some time, which gave him a sense of direction, but he could not remember where his childhood home was. Was it south of that sign? North? East or west? Springfield was a large city, so he could be five minutes away or fifty minutes away. He needed more information.

As he dug further down, he realized that he was not going to find the answer that he was looking for. He had unearthed only the most generic relics of suburban living—a few broken mobile phones, a running shoe, a baby stroller with a convertible car seat, some cheap clothing from brands that he remembered seeing in shop windows when there used to be malls. Nothing of importance, and certainly nothing that would tell him where exactly he was.

He knew that he had a good shot of walking north to find someone. There had been reports from days prior of people still living in, or roaming near, the major city centers. He did not know what he would come across, but he knew that any situation was better than trying to survive alone. The end of the world was too sudden, and all of his friends had scattered, were too far, now gone to him. The voices would call out to him.

Why didn't you know anyone around you?

You couldn't you try to make just one new friend?

He started to think about all the missed opportunities. The birthday parties that he skipped because he was working. The family vacation that was postponed because the thought of Peter running his project drove him mad. A project that clearly did not have any value anymore. Moments spent ruminating over every decision had turned into hours of inaction because he felt he needed to control even minor things. The time he spent schmoozing and kissing up to those overpaid managers just for the chance to get more work and spend less time living his life. And when he found time to see his wife and child, he frantically checked his phone every minute, waiting for the next big update, the next opportunity to jump into action. He would always snap when they asked him to join the party. Always another email. Always another crisis averted. Or at least, what he considered to be a crisis at the time.

The contempt he had each day for everyone and everything. The resentment that he had for his career because it took him away from his family. The resentment that he had for his family because they took him away from his career. The stress put upon him, the stress he put upon himself, and how meaningless it all was in the end.

There was a glimmer in the distance, a slight twinkle against the horizon, or was it a person approaching? Could this be it? Would the Wanderer have to wander no more? He mustered up his strength and stumbled hurriedly towards the silhouette. The sand and dirt felt lighter and seemed to smoothly flow outward as he kicked and shuffled. He squinted through the haze, trying to assess whether the person in the distance was friend or foe.

What is that glimmer? Is it a gun? Is it a knife? Is it a watch? Too hard to tell...

The figure just stood there, staring at him. There was no movement, no flinching, no beckoning to others even to signal a trap. The person in the distance was disciplined and stoic. The Wanderer kept moving. He had no other option.

He started to see the figure more clearly. What had looked like a dark shadow bloomed into something horrific. Its skin was gray, which was more shocking against the bright blue dress it wore with white polka dots and a white satin ribbon around the waist. It was a woman! He mustered more strength to rush to her.

She could be injured. She could be in distress. Why does she look like that? Is she dead?

The sun was getting hotter, and the air was getting thicker. His lungs felt heavier. The sand around him kicked up. He was the architect of his own suffocation. He had to push through if it meant finding someone to join with. The woman's skin was grayer and drier than he suspected, and she was missing hair. He could not make out her features, so he could glean her condition. He could only focus on that bright blue dress.

Where have I seen that dress before? Do I know this woman?

Soon he was upon her. As he neared her, a gust of wind knocked the woman down. Her body slid toward a small dune. He thought he heard her head slam against something hard, like a rock, so he pushed forward with all his strength. At last, he made it to her and grabbed her bare foot. Stiff as a board. She was dead. He shuffled slowly toward her to see who she was when he saw that her skin had the look of plastic, dull and cracked. He realized that it did not just look like plastic... it *was* plastic. She was a mannequin.

The Wanderer let out an exasperated sigh. He had pushed himself, chased against hope, only to be disappointed by a fashionable lump. He stood the mannequin up to observe anything that could give him information. He remembered where he had seen this dress. He and his wife had seen it in a small independent shop. They were talking about plans for an upcoming vacation. The dress could have been used for a wide range of events—cocktail parties, wedding receptions, cruises, bar crawls, any event where they would spend time out with friends. She remarked how lovely the dress would look on her. It was true, she would have looked beautiful with that dress against her long, dark, curly hair and curvy frame. The memory made him sad. He missed his wife so much.

But this gave him an opportunity, bigger than he was expecting. The store where the mannequin was located had been in the central hub of Springfield, and there was only one location for that particular store. Also, they used a mannequin, unlike the standalone stores that were nearby, where they dressed special T-shaped poles to show their merchandise without taking a lot of space. He now knew where he was—he was near the mall. He gathered his thoughts and whatever breath he had left and searched for ways to get into that mall.

He started looking for depressions in the sand, areas where the land might dip from roofs, windows, or doorways. He grabbed at different indents in the ground, but each handful felt as dense as anywhere else. He slid a few times down a sand dune, closing in on his goal, but his efforts led to dead ends only. He knew he was getting closer though. He kept finding other objects—hand mirrors, combs, baby bottles, men's sneakers, collared shirts, broken couch legs. Everything indicated that there had been plenty of foot traffic in this area. He continued descending into different paths until he could feel hot pavement beneath the sand. He had reached the end of a descent that felt like the lowest level of an inferno. At that bottom level, he began to tunnel through walls of sand around him, careful not to trap himself too deep. This proved difficult as winds blew across his position and flooded his mouth and clothes with more and more sand. He felt the weight of earth closing around him. He needed to act quickly, to find something to save his life.

This can't be the end.

What are we going to do?

How will I get out? How will we get out?

As he made one last effort, his left hand scraped against something small and rectangular with different jutting edges. He grabbed it and pulled, but it was stuck in sand and string. He thrust his right hand towards the object. There were knots tied to different points on the object. He fiddled with the strings but pulling only caused more sand to pour down around him. The sand started to fill his shoes and pile around his ankles. He was not going to give up.

Yes, I got one of the strings off. The sand was up to his knees.

I just need to tug on it a little harder. More sand piled around him, halfway up his thighs now.

I've almost got it.

The sand was at his waist, filling his pockets, trapping the lower half of his body. He ignored it. He had a feeling that whatever he was grabbing was going to bring his salvation. He pulled harder and harder. His fingers worked and worked until the object was finally free.

Finally!

It was a walkie-talkie used by security guards, with one percent of its battery power. He did not have a lot of time. He pulled his arms up to shoulder height—the sand had trapped most of his body and winds were pushing more in from above. He twisted the walkie-talkie knobs trying to find a channel that still worked. The feeds were full of static, but he kept trying different combinations hoping he'd hear something. He lifted the radio higher and higher as sand piled up around him. He began to realize that he might not survive. Finally, when the sand had almost buried his whole body, he found one working channel. But it didn't matter. His mouth and nose were covered now. He could not speak. All that remained was to hear the last message, cold and robotic, before his breathing ceased and everything went dark.

"Hello. We're contacting you about your car's service warranty…"

Lost Connection

"I'm not so sure."

Juliana still had reservations about undergoing the procedure. "What if something goes wrong?"

Her boyfriend, Dexter, was reassuring but slightly exasperated. "Babe, I thought we talked about it. They said the risk was very low."

Dr. Sampson who was seated, writing on her clipboard, and avoiding eye contact, interjected. "It's true. The procedure is still experimental, and the known side effects aren't too serious. However, the chance that any of these things happen is practically zero."

Juliana was not convinced. "And remind me again, what were some of those side effects?"

"Of the hundreds of subjects that we implanted successfully, one suffered some temporary blurred vision that cleared up in a matter of days, and one became slightly drowsy. And in that case, we administered a mild stimulant at a regular time each day, which did the trick. It's a small price to pay for such cutting-edge research."

"And these are the *known* side effects... what about the unknown ones?"

Dr. Sampson raised her head slightly and rolled her eyes above her glasses to look at Juliana directly. "Ms. Cortez, if I could tell you about the unknown side effects, then they wouldn't be *unknown*, now would they?"

Juliana folded her arms and slumped down after being made a fool for her question.

"Jules, I know this seems like a lot, but I think this is going to be good for us. I know I haven't been perfect, and I want to prove that I trust you more than anyone, to give you everything—including the chance to see the world through my eyes."

Dexter was not exaggerating. The procedure in question was to insert synchronized ocular implants, allowing both patients to see what the other sees at the flick of a switch no larger than the tip of a human thumb. "Doctor, can you tell us more about how it works so that she can feel better about it?"

"Yes, Mr. Baines. That was going to be part of our closeout procedures today. And while everything you need to know is outlined in the countless and exhaustive release forms that you have signed and the package that you will receive in your email after we complete our session today, I will also give you a brief rundown now." Dr. Sampson flipped some pages on her clipboard to a one-page script and began reading in a monotone fashion.

"The goal of CFX Biotech, and its subsidiaries and affiliates, is to connect all of humankind through one sensory mind. As an early adopter of the future of humankind, you will receive our newest and most advanced ocular implant, known as the Binary Star. The Binary Star is actually two ocular implants that were programmed and manufactured together, allowing the implants to share a joint connection. This joint connection will allow both users to, at the click of a button, replace their own visual field with the visual field of the user with the other associated implant. Each implant is inserted near the back of the subject's head and connects to the user's occipital lobe. This allows for minimal lag in response time, and connectivity through a wireless radio network with a band dedicated to that specific set of implants. The materials used to manufacture the implants are cased in inert materials to remove any risk of contamination or decay and follow guidelines beyond the highest recommended requirements. There are also security measures built into both the devices and the networks which exceed those of even the most secure, publicly known networks in the world. Welcome to the wonderful future of tomorrow. Results may vary."

Dr. Sampson flipped her working notes over the script and continued writing.

"Jules, what do you think?"

She hesitated. "I mean, it seems like it could be okay."

Dexter smiled. "That's what I'm talking about." He leaned over and hugged Juliana tightly. She returned his pressure tentatively from beneath his firm embrace and patted his back lightly.

"Now then, Mr. Baines, Ms. Cortez. Shall we proceed?"

Four months later, Dexter and Juliana arrived for their follow-up appointment. Dr. Sampson sat emotionless, taking notes during their check-in. "So it seems things are going well?"

Dexter cleared his throat before speaking. "Well, first, we want to thank you for all of the assistance after the implant surgery."

"It's not a problem, Mr. Baines. That's part of our protocol."

"Yes, we read that in your package and we know that it's standard. Still, we didn't realize how much it would change our lives."

Juliana interjected. "It's true. All of the food delivery and private chefs and home repairs and new furniture. Even the new artwork in the house is so beautiful. This isn't something we could have afforded without you."

"Well, you do so much for us. We get such good information from all of our subjects, and you all have been very diligent about staying stable and healthy and following our instructions. Quite frankly, that's more than we could say for some of our previous subjects. Not that we expected much from the others, but you both remained fastidious."

Dexter agreed. "Thank you, Dr. Sampson."

"And I trust that the additional monetary compensation was adequate?"

"More than adequate. It helped us get out of a pretty large hole, so we've been able to really start planning for our future. Maybe even getting better, more stable careers and not having to jump from job to job all the time. Definitely some breathing room."

Sampson continued taking notes without lifting her head. She recorded their responses. "Excellent. And how has day-to-day function been?"

"Our daily work has been amazing," Juliana said. "For example, I'm usually the one that cooks, because I enjoy doing it for myself and I'm more aware of where everything is in the kitchen. But sometimes, I'm tired or I want to have some time to myself, so I started using the Binary Star to guide him through making some basic meals. And because it's an easier process with me guiding him, he's been more enthusiastic about doing it, so now I can help him while I'm out of the house running errands or visiting friends."

"Excellent, Ms. Cortez. And for you, Mr. Baines, have you felt the same?"

"Oh, very much. Like with the cooking, I like to fix things around the house, but I get tired too, or I have to practice my bass or go to my band rehearsals. I would have to wait until the weekend or when I could find some time, but now I can help Juliana fix things that she was nervous about touching. So we've been able to help each other a lot."

"It's been great for helping us connect and lessening the burden on each other." Juliana's voice and demeanor were warm.

The doctor continued writing. "This is certainly good news for everyone." She completed a sentence and looks up from her notes. "And how is your intimacy?"

Without controlling it, Dexter smiled and nodded his head.

Juliana started blushing. "Well, things are so much more... interesting."

"Please elaborate." Sampson was straightforward but stopped taking notes.

"It's become so much more interesting. We've been able to... body swap."

"Body swap?"

"Not necessarily body swap. More like, just being able to see ourselves through each other's eyes while we do it. It's just so intense. We can guide each other and find new pleasure centers and positions. When we look deep into each other's eyes, we can also see ourselves. It's wonderful." Juliana sighed. Dexter remained silent, a sly grin on his face.

"So being able to shift vision, it has led to a more... sensory experience."

Dexter and Juliana said at the same time, "Yes."

Dr. Sampson started writing notes again. "That's wonderful." She remained emotionless in her analysis. "Well, everything looks like it's within our expected outcomes and scenarios. I think things are moving in the right direction." She tore a piece of paper from her notepad and handed it to Juliana. "Please take this to the receptionist so that we can schedule your next follow-up session. It should be scheduled within the next six months. Whatever date the receptionist provides, that date cannot be missed and cannot be rescheduled, neither before nor after that date. Please ensure that you clear your schedule to make sure that the meeting date is honored. If the date is not honored, we cannot guarantee that we can continue further support beyond the network use of the Binary Star implants."

Juliana took the note and put it in her purse. "Alright, we'll make sure to do whatever is necessary. Thank you, Dr. Sampson."

"Yes, thank you Doctor." Dexter and Juliana stood up and walked out. Dr. Sampson remained in her seat as they left her office, nonchalantly scribbling her notes.

Juliana was at her desk, fiddling with a spreadsheet trying to confirm her numbers for her calculations, when her boss walked up to her cubicle.

"Jules, can you get those numbers ready in the next few minutes? Tory is going on vacation tomorrow, and I want to make sure her team has all our information cleared before we present this week."

"Yes, Bill, I'm almost done. I want to make sure these last few columns are adding right."

"Great, thanks. I know I can count on you. And no need for me to review them, you can send them straight to Tory once you think they're good. I trust you."

"Thanks, Bill. Now, is this for the meeting with the vice-presidents, senior vice-presidents, executive vice-presidents, executive directors, or senior executive directors?" She spoke a bit loudly and emphasized each job title.

"Now, Jules, don't start."

"Or did they create a new set of VPs or directors while I was preparing this?"

Bill chuckled. "Jules, please don't. You're going to ruin the whole operation. Also, I don't know who's going to be at the meeting. So I would leave it alone and just send everything along."

"Will do, thanks." Bill walked back to his office and closed the door as Juliana put the finishing touches on her work and emailed them.

There seemed to be a never-ending rotation of Chief Something Officers who required briefings and a confusing mess of bureaucracy that never went anywhere for her. She had a hard time justifying why she was receiving a paycheck or even going into the office each day. It was a slog, but it kept her busy. She entered one last number into her spreadsheet and then sent the file to Tory. Once she confirmed the file was sent, she pulled her company badge from a slot in her computer, grabbed her purse, and left her cubicle for lunch.

Juliana sat by herself in the cafeteria on the tenth floor of the building. Normally she brought prepared food from home, but that day she had had a particularly tough time getting out of bed and accidentally left her lunch on the kitchen counter. As she shoveled another forkful of under-seasoned penne into her mouth, she thought about what Dexter was doing at that moment. Maybe he was working on that novel he was writing? Was he learning another instrument? Painting another landscape? She thought about how talented he was and how keen he was on finding inspiration in everything. His artistic vision was what drew her to him in the first place, and she was frequently blown away by what he created.

She wanted to surprise him with something special, so she slid her hand into her pocket and pressed the small button on her controller to see what he was doing. Instantly, she was transported away from her uninspired meal to his creative process. Only, he was not in the middle of an artistic breakthrough or laboring over his canvas. Rather, she saw through his eyes, as he was hunched over his phone, staring at Internet models. Beautiful, buxom models scrolled past his social media feeds. Juliana was surprised. She was not upset—the women were clearly beautiful—but the whole scene was jarring. She saw her partner as such as force, a combination of admirable traits and raw physical attraction. She did not consider that he would have such base, mundane urges. After seeing some admittedly amazing figures, she pressed her controller button and reverted to her own eyesight. She finished her bland food, purchased a cookie from the baked goods section, and then went back to her desk to finish the rest of her workday.

Juliana arrived home just after six o'clock in the evening, carrying dinner in several plastic bags. She typed in the house code into the newly installed keypad lock for the front door and walked in.

"Hey Dex, I'm home!" She closed the door behind her with her foot.

"Hey love! I'm in the living room!" Juliana walked into the living room to see Dexter staring at a blend of vibrant blues and deep greens splattered across an extra-large canvas laid on top of an even larger gray plastic tarp. "I'm thinking about doing some kind of abstract landscape thing but with throwing all the paint, rather than using paintbrushes. What do you think?"

"I think it's going to look as great as all the other ones." She kissed one of the few spots on his cheek that was not caked with paint.

"You're too sweet." He looked at the bags she was carrying and sniffed the air. "What did you bring?"

"I picked up some Greek food for dinner. I got some gyro meat with rice, spanakopita, and a few pieces of baklava for dessert."

"Sounds delightful. Thanks love."

"No problem. I just want to make sure we get the food to the refrigerator if we're not going to eat it." She walked the food into the kitchen and divided the food across two plates. Then she sat down at the dinner table and watched videos on her phone. Dexter continued his work in the living room for an additional fifteen minutes before wiping the sweat from his face, washing his hands, and joining Juliana for dinner. His face and clothes still had paint smudges.

As they sat together talking about their respective days and enjoying the flavors dancing on their tongues, Dexter could see that Juliana was holding back.

"Tell me, love, you look like you want to say something."

Juliana tried to play coy. "What do you mean, Dex?"

"Come on, something's going on. It looks like something is on your mind."

"Well, I didn't want to bring it up, because it's not really a big deal."

Dexter smirked. "It seems like it's big enough of a deal. Out with it."

She relaxed her shoulders and took a deep breath. "Okay, well, I didn't want to tell you because it seems like it's a bit extra. I... I used my controller when I was having lunch today."

Dexter's smirk slipped from his face. "Oh yeah? What did you see?"

"I saw you scrolling through your phone. Just looking at a bunch of girls."

"Oh. Yeah, I was taking a break and looking through my feed."

"I know, that's why I didn't want to say anything. It's not that serious. Plus, some of them looked very... comfy."

"Ha! Yeah, maybe a couple. A lot of those just came up because of the algorithm. I liked a couple of the pictures, then all of a sudden that's all my feed starts showing me." He grabbed her hand gently. "I promise, love, I'll do better and not look at that stuff on my phone.”

Juliana smiled playfully. “Just on your phone?”

Dexter laughed. “Okay, okay, I won’t look at that stuff at all.”

“I’m glad we talked about it. Like I said, it’s not a big deal. I should probably stop carrying the switch around so much. It’s too tempting.”

“Don’t worry about it, love. I don’t have anything to hide. Except for a few big booties every once in a while.”

They both laughed. Then, they kissed. Then, they left the kitchen for the bedroom. The food never made it to the refrigerator.

Dexter could not shake the feeling of betrayal, even three days after Juliana told him about her intrusion. In the moment, he was honestly alright, but as the idea settled into his mind, other thoughts ate away at him.

Has she done this before?

Weren’t we going to talk about it every time we used it?

What makes me think she isn’t going to do it again?

His thoughts chipped away at his core. He did appreciate that, without the distraction of internet models, he had produced so much quality artistic work over those three days of rumination. But he still entertained the idea of getting back at her. He decided that he could intrude a bit himself, that he could show her what it feels like to skulk through her eyes without her knowing. So, he did just that.

During daytime breaks for several weeks, he sat on the couch and pressed his controller button to see what she was looking at throughout the day. On some days, he would see only her work screens. On other days, he would catch her during a daytime yoga class. He would watch the other women through her eyes, which slowly replaced his need to scroll through feeds of beautiful women on social media. He would sometimes see the street from her perspective as she walked and notice how other men, and occasionally women, would look at her as she strutted down the sidewalk. He took some pride in the fact that others saw how beautiful Juliana was, but he was still uncomfortable with the more obvious or egregious looks.

Dexter felt bad about abusing his access, but he learned more about Juliana every day. It made him love her even more. He was more affectionate in the morning, gentler in the evening. In turn, Juliana felt safer and became more relaxed, more encouraging even beyond her usual support. This only led him to use his controller more.

Still, he fluctuated between feelings of deep connection and even deeper insecurity. When he was not watching her, he was thinking about what she was doing. On top of that, he became hyper-concerned about whether she was checking on him again. He spent more time sitting on the couch or continuously working without breaks. He whipped between intense moments of productivity and dragging malaise and paranoia. Juliana had no clue. Or at least, she never indicated that she did.

After another spicy lovemaking session one night, Juliana rolled over to go to sleep. "Sorry, love, I don't want to cuddle tonight. I'm really tired and I need to be up early."

Dexter looked down toward his waist. "But I'm still up *now*."

She giggled and swiped back to smack him. "Dex, stop. I have to sleep."

"Alright, alright. But you're not gonna at least brush your teeth?"

"You know, that's a good point." Juliana rolled out of bed and walked to the bathroom, dressed in a loose T-shirt and one of Dexter's pairs of blue boxer shorts. He casually reached for his controller that was sitting on his nightstand and pressed. He looked at Juliana's reflection through her eyes—a stunning sight. She was sweaty and her hair was messy, and he stared at her curves. Suddenly the allure slipped away as she bent over the sink to spit her toothpaste out. Dexter quickly closed his eyes. He wanted to keep the magic alive. He reached back to his controller to press the button again and bring back his own vision before she walked back to her side of the bed.

Juliana let out a big yawn. "Oof, I'm so tired. Good night, love."

"Good night." Dexter reached over to the lamp on his nightstand and tugged gently on the lamp. He then reached down for his silk eye mask. He had a habit of opening his eyes at the slightest disturbance of light and needed reinforcement. Once he put on his mask, he rolled to his right and went to sleep. He did not realize that when he reached for the eye mask that he had accidentally grazed the ocular switch with the lower part of his hand. His eyes were already closed, and Juliana fell asleep almost immediately.

Dexter woke up late. Juliana left for work early to get a start on a big project, so he took more time for rest and planning out his next project.

He looked for his phone while still half asleep and the eye mask still on. He bumped the controller again without realizing. He was a bit startled, so he took off the eye mask and checked his vision to make sure he did not trigger anything. A fantasy, he thought. Nothing but his own eyes working.

After shaking off the sleepy feeling and brushing his teeth, Dexter went to the kitchen for a cup of coffee and a bowl of cereal. He sat at the table sketching his next painting. Suddenly, he saw something flash in front of him from left to right. He saw red and blue lights fly across the room. He scrunched his face in confusion, then looked around to see if anything flew past. Nothing. He looked out the window to see if he had inadvertently caught a glimpse of a police car driving by. Nothing. He went around the first floor and looked at all of the light bulbs to see if anything burned out and created a weird visual effect. Still nothing. "That's weird," he muttered to himself. He left it alone and went back to sketching his day.

A few seconds later, he saw a faint white circle floating before him, perched near the bottom of his visual field. This one did not go away so quickly. The circle looked ethereal, hovering just on the edge of his visual periphery. As much as he looked down, it just wouldn't go away.

"Wait, what is going on?"

He started seeing other floating, transparent objects floating through the room. He saw colors. He saw more things slip by. He saw what he thought were people.

"What's happening? Am I seeing ghosts? This can't be."

Either this had something to do with the implants, or he was starting to lose his mind. He knew he had to call Dr. Sampson immediately to find out what had happened. He went to the bedroom and rifled through his things until he found the card that she had given them. Then he pulled out his phone and called the number. A receptionist picked up the phone on the other end.

"Good morning, CFX Biotech. Dr. Sampson's office. How may I help you?"

"Uh, hello. My name is Dexter Baines, I'm a patient of Dr. Sampson's."

"Alright, Mr. Baines, how can I assist you?"

"Yes, um, I'm calling because I'm having some trouble with the ocular implant that Dr. Sampson helped us get. I'm starting to see things."

"Well wasn't that the point of the operation, Mr. Baines?"

Dexter was taken aback at the receptionist's condescension. "I mean, I can see things. It's just that I'm starting to see more than my own vision, even when I'm not pressing the button."

"Ah, I see. That makes more sense. Thank you for clarifying. I will check to see if Dr. Sampson is in her office and patch you through. If she does not pick up for some reason, please leave her a voicemail and someone will get back to you."

"Thank you, sir. I'll be sure to—"

Before he could finish, the receptionist transferred the call to Dr. Sampson's line.

He said "hello" into the line a few times before another voice chimed.

"Good morning, this is Dr. Sampson. How may I assist you?"

Dexter was nervous but proceeded. "Good morning, Dr. Sampson. This is Dexter Baines, one of your patients."

"Ah, yes, Mr. Baines. How may I help you today?"

"Well, I'm having a problem with the implant. I'm starting to see things that aren't there. They look like—"

"Phantoms?"

"Yes, exactly. How did you know?"

"It's a common occurrence in our subjects. Occasionally, our subjects find it best to overuse their implants. We refer to them as 'phantoms,' though that's technically not what is happening."

"Oh. I see."

"Tell me, when did they start happening?"

"Just this morning, after I woke up."

"And what was the longest amount of time you were using your implant prior to the phantoms?"

"Not very long. I haven't even been awake for an hour."

"Are you sure, Mr. Baines? Not even an hour? It's almost eleven o'clock." Dr. Sampson was being as condescending as the receptionist.

"Doctor, I can assure you that—"

"Yes, of course, Mr. Baines. I just want to get a clear gauge of what is happening. Typically, these things happen later in the day. Our subjects may be a little too insecure in their partner's whereabouts, or maybe their partner is on an extended overnight trip and they want to be part of whatever they're doing at the time. There was one instance where a person turned theirs on and fell asleep on the couch. They had their implant functioning for at least 45 minutes straight. Good thing their eyes were closed, or they could have risked damaging their optic nerve."

That last story triggered Dexter's memory. *Did I hit the button before I went to bed?* He stayed silent while trying to recall his sleep routine the night before.

"Mr. Baines, are you there?"

"Yes, Doctor. I'm trying to think of what happened last night. It's possible that I might have... done that thing you were just talking about."

"What thing?"

"The falling asleep thing."

"You mean taking a nap?"

Dexter started to feel embarrassed. "Well, not a nap. It's possible that I might have hit the button on my controller before I went to bed last night."

Dr. Sampson hesitated a moment before answering. "Mr. Baines, how long were you asleep for?"

"Well, we went to bed, I think, around eleven thirty."

"And what time did you say you woke up today?"

"Just after ten o'clock."

Dr. Sampson hesitated again. "I see."

"Is that bad?"

"Well, Mr. Baines, if you refer to the materials that we provided for you, you will notice that the implants are not to be operated for more than one hour at any given time, and that they require some cooldown time in between sessions. Tell me, Mr. Baines, did you read the entire package when we gave it to you."

Dexter was feeling more embarrassed through the conversation. "I didn't. I thought I caught that, but I guess I missed it."

"Well, Mr. Baines, hopefully the damage isn't too great. You were asleep, so it may not be permanent."

He was taken aback. "Wait, it's possible that this could be permanent?"

Dr. Sampson was unmoved. "I'm not sure, Mr. Baines. We will need to bring you in for a diagnostic check to make sure that everything is working as intended."

"Okay, no problem. I can come in any time today or tomorrow."

"Mr. Baines, it's not that simple. There are protocols and paperwork. We need to bring in the proper technicians who are familiar with your particular model, and we need to inform our legal counsel on your return to the facility."

"Alright, when is the earliest that you can see me?"

"Again, I'm not sure, Mr. Baines. I will transfer you back to the receptionist."

"Sure, that works. Thank you, Dr. Samp—" Again, he was cut off.

The receptionist came back on the line. "Good morning, CFX Biotech. Dr. Sampson's office. How may I help you?"

"Hello again, this is Dexter Baines."

"Alright, Mr. Baines, how can I assist you?"

Dexter was feeling déjà vu. "So, I just spoke with Dr. Sampson about scheduling a diagnostic check."

"Okay, let me check her availability." Dexter heard computer typing in the background. "Mr. Baines, Dr. Sampson is available exactly two weeks from today."

"Oh, no, that can't be. I'm having a serious issue here. I can't wait that long."

"I'm sorry, Mr. Baines, that's the earliest availability. She is quite busy."

Dexter sighed. "Alright, I can take that appointment. Is it possible to get on some sort of waitlist if something opens up?"

"Yes, Mr. Baines, we can put you on a waitlist and reach out if we have anything come up. Thank you."

"Sounds good. Thank y—" The receptionist hung up.

That afternoon, Juliana came home early to have lunch with Dexter. This time, she brought home Indonesian food from a small café near her office. As they sat in the kitchen enjoying delicious chicken satay, Dexter nervously thought about what he was seeing. At times throughout the morning, there would be flashes of ghostly wandering, but the flashes were never consistent. He debated internally whether he should even mention it to Juliana.

If I tell her, should I tell her now? When should I bother?

If I don't tell her, what will happen if this happens again?

He decided to keep it from her for the time being and wanted to enjoy his meal and talk to his partner.

"So, love, what brought you home so early?"

"Oh, today has just been crazy. I was running a bit behind and wasn't paying attention, and I almost got hit by a police car."

"That's awful!"

"I know! I was fine, so it wasn't a problem. Someone pulled me back, and they were very nice. But then I was really hungry, so I grabbed some street food. It was just awful."

"Oh yeah?"

"Yeah, and they served it on one of those terrible, flimsy white paper plates, so I almost spilled it on myself. They didn't even bother putting a double plate."

"Problems on top of problems."

"Exactly!"

Dexter grimaced. "So did you make it to work safely?"

"Yeah, it was fine. But Bill was on some bullshit again, so I decided to finish the rest of the day here. Don't worry, I'm going to stay upstairs while you work."

"It's cool, Jules. You can be wherever. I can focus with my headphones on."

"Cool. I'm still going to work upstairs, though." She stood up to get a small plate and a large glass. "Actually, I think I'm going to grab some things to go." She poured water into the glass and scooped some of the food onto the plate. "Let me know if you need anything else." She kissed Dexter on the cheek and walked away with her food and drink.

"Sure thing. Love you." Dexter stayed seated in the kitchen eating his meal.

He took a bite of his curry dish, losing himself in his creative thoughts. Several minutes later, he saw a bright light appear in the center of his field of vision. Not a clear light—rather, a dim, rectangular box of light hovering in front of him like a glowing portal into heaven.

"Not again."

He stopped eating and tried to focus on what was happening. Small shadowy spots dashed across the light, moving from corner to corner. The light tilted and shifted, bouncing and dancing, jostling and sliding.

"What is happening?"

He stood up from the table to find Juliana, who was sitting on their bed and working on her laptop.

"Hey love, what are you doing?"

"Oh, I'm just working on *another* presentation for *another* meeting."

Dexter walked to her and gave her a hug and a kiss. "Quick question. How is your implant working?"

"It's fine, nothing has been bothering me. Why do you ask?"

"No reason, I just wanted to ask." He could see her as he looked down, but a faint glow framed her face. "Just wanted to know if you needed to get anything checked out."

Juliana looked concerned. "Is something going on with yours?"

"Oh no, no. Mine is cool. Just making sure in case I needed to make an appointment."

"Okay, well if anything happens, let me know. I want to make sure that everything is going smoothly."

"Sure thing." As Dexter shifted to leave the room, he tripped on the laptop charging cable. The laptop flew from Juliana's lap and crashed to the floor.

"Oh no!" Juliana moved quickly to pick up the laptop. "I hope everything is alright." She checked the screen and casing. "Okay, it looks like everything is working fine. Nothing's broken."

Dexter noticed something weird. When he tripped over the laptop, the bright light dropped from his sight, in the same direction and manner as the laptop. But just as quickly as the light went away, it returned to him when Juliana picked up the laptop and turned the screen on again.

"Dex!" Dexter was startled as Juliana was trying to speak to him. "Are you okay?"

"Uh, yes, why?"

"I was just asking you if are alright. I thought the laptop landed on your foot or something."

"Oh, sorry. No, everything is fine. It missed me." He was hesitant as he realized that he zoned out for a bit.

"That's good. But love, just be more careful." She was a bit annoyed but compassionate.

"I will. Sorry about that." He walked out of the bedroom. "I love you."

"Love you, too."

As he polished off his plate of curry Dexter thought about that bright box of light that appeared before. He felt more anxious about the implant, about what these phantoms meant. Then, he considered another option.

"Am I seeing what Juliana is seeing?"

He thought about his earlier conversations with Juliana and what was going on that day. Juliana was working on her computer and Dexter was looking at a bright, glowing box. When the computer fell, the box slipped away as well, in the same direction and in the same manner.

The laptop screen? Was that her laptop screen?

He then thought about the conversation he had had with Juliana about her day.

The red and blue lights. The white circle.

The police car and the plate of food.

Is this really happening?

Suddenly, he started seeing another phantom. The visual cues were hard to make out, so he decided to test his theory. He called up to Juliana.

"Hey love?"

He heard her response from upstairs. "Yeah?"

"I think something got on my hand from the food. Can you check your hand to see if you got anything on you?"

He stared deeply, and there it was. A faint outline of Juliana's hand, moving back and forth. The palm of her hand, then the back of her hand.

"I don't see anything!"

He was dumbstruck. He was seeing a dim version of what she could see without pressing the button. His voice trembled slightly.

"Thanks love!"

"That was weird, but you're welcome!"

He went to the table where he placed his controller earlier that day and activated the button. Nothing. He pressed it repeatedly. Nothing. He held the button down and closed his eyes, hoping that it would reset the system. Still nothing.

He sat on the couch and took a deep breath. His mind was racing.

What am I going to do? How can I wait until the appointment? How can I keep this from Juliana?

He took deep breaths to keep from passing out. He calmed himself, then lay down for a brief nap, hoping it would help clear his mind. He wanted to keep his eyes closed until he could come up with a better plan.

He woke up several hours later in the dark living room, confused and groggy. Only a few slivers of light sone through the windows. The house felt even quieter than usual, as if the world had ceased to move. Fortunately, in the shadows, he did not see any projections from Juliana's vision. He searched around until he could find his phone, which showed an unread text message. He swiped down on the phone screen to see a preview, which read:

[Juliana (7:42 pm) hey love, saw you asleep. went out to meet a friend. be back later.]

He was not aware that she was meeting a friend that night. Dexter was curious, but he wanted to refrain from using his controller. The malfunction was becoming an ordeal, and he knew that if he let his curiosity get to him, he would be consumed by it. So, he texted back:

[(8:49 pm) just woke up. thanks for letting me know. see you in a bit.]

She instantly sent back a heart emoji.

Dexter walked to the wall and turned on the lights. He had not given himself enough time to prepare for what came next. The visions were no longer faint glimmers. Rather, they had become even clearer and more pronounced than before. He could see Juliana's view overlaying his own, like a photograph with double exposure. He could see people walking through the walls of his house. He could see Juliana texting and reading on her phone in between conversations with her friends, as well as a man he had never met before. They were laughing. She and her friends were very touchy, caressing each other's arms and shoulders whenever they told jokes. Including the man that he had not met.

Paranoia kicked in. *She said she was meeting a friend. Is he the friend? Who is that? Is she trying to cheat on me? She better not be.* Dexter called her. He could see her pick up her phone and look at it, showing "Dex" on the front as it rang. She looked at it briefly, then silenced her phone and put it away. Dexter went from paranoid to angry. There was not much he could do before she got home, so he stewed in his jealousy and rage. Without other options, he called Dr. Sampson's office again to see if he could schedule his appointment sooner.

"Good evening, CFX Biotech. Dr. Sampson's office. How may I help you?"

"This is Dexter Baines. I called earlier about my appointment."

"Yes, Mr. Baines, how can I assist you?"

Dexter was indignant. "Did you hear anything about an updated appointment? "

The receptionist remained calm, the sound of his keys clacking in the background as he typed. "Let me check... I'm sorry, Mr. Baines. Unfortunately, we have not had any cancellations since you called us this morning."

"Well, when can I hear back?" Dexter's voice was rising, trembling with emotion.

"Mr. Baines, unfortunately, I can't answer that for you. Have there been any changes since we spoke this morning?"

Dexter brought down his voice to answer. "Yes, sir. The phantoms are getting worse. They're starting to get more detailed and are starting to bleed into my own vision."

"Have you tried pressing the button to reset your vision?"

"I tried that. It doesn't work."

"Have you tried taking a nap or having any sort of prolonged eye closure?"

"I just woke up from a nap. I didn't even know that was one of things I could do."

"Mr. Baines, I assure you it was part of your package."

"Don't talk to me about that now!" Dexter could not keep his cool.

"My apologies, Mr. Baines, I'm just asking questions to make sure I understand how best to support you."

"Fine. Then what else can I do?"

"One more question. Can you tell me what you see right now? And please be as descriptive as possible."

"Well, I'm sitting in my living room, so I can see the walls and pictures, and my couch and my art supplies. But I can also see my wife spending time with her friends. A lot of people are around, a bunch of women... and a man next to her." He choked up when he referenced the man. "I can see the table in front of her with lots of drinks around. Some food too. I can see a bunch of people walking around in the background like they're floating past everyone. I can see another... "

"Alright, Mr. Baines, I think I understand the general issue. Let me see if I can transfer you." The phone line clicked to another dial tone. Dexter thought about what he was going to say to Dr. Sampson to communicate the issue. Suddenly, the dial tone switched back.

"Hello, Mr. Baines?" The receptionist, not Dr. Sampson, responded on the line.

"Yes? Is Dr. Sampson there?"

"Unfortunately, Mr. Baines, Dr. Sampson is not available this evening. Furthermore, we are no longer able to further provide support to either you or Ms. Cortez at this time."

Dexter could not believe what he had just heard. "I'm sorry, could you please repeat that?"

"Mr. Baines, we can no longer provide support to you. You are not required to return any of the equipment to CFX Biotech. We have received any diagnostic information to continue our mission, and we thank you for the information provided."

"Wait, you can't be serious. Please get the doctor on the phone call."

"I'm sorry, Mr. Baines. I am not able to do that at this time. Thank you for your support, and we wish you well."

"Hey, stop that. Stop that! Get Dr. Sampson on the phone now! Get her..."

The phone clicked. There was only silence from the other end.

"No, no, no, no, NO!" He quickly tapped the call button on his phone to retrieve the number and dial back. After a few rings, he heard an automated message:

"The number that you are trying to reach is no longer in service. Please hang up and try your call again."

Again, he tried to call the same number. And again, he received the same message. Again, and again, the same issue.

Dexter let out a guttural scream into the phone! No one responded on the other line, and Juliana's vision took over more and more of his. He saw that she was getting into her car, so he called her. Finally, she answered.

"Hey love, what up?"

"Hey! Where are you?" Dexter could not hide his agitation.

"Uh, I'm just getting into the car and heading home."

"Why are you coming home so late?"

"Babe, I wasn't even out that long. What's going on? Are you okay?"

"Yeah, I'm fine. When are you getting home?"

"I don't know, I guess in about twenty minutes." She accelerated toward a yellow light but decided to slow down.

"Good job babe, don't run that, just be safe."

Juliana was surprised. "Wait, how did you know that I didn't run the light? Are you plugged into me right now?"

"No, my controller isn't even on."

"Then how do you know where I am, Dex?"

Dexter did not have a good answer. He failed to tell her about his failing implant, but he had no other option. But he still tried to save face. "My implant isn't working, Jules. I think we're both using our controllers too much."

"That's not possible, Dex."

"How do you know, Jules?"

"Dex, I haven't used my controller since I accidentally pressed it on you that one time."

"Wait, really?"

"Yes, I left it in the top drawer in the kitchen. Haven't touched it since."

Dexter ran to the kitchen and checked the top drawer. There was nothing there.

"Jules, I'm not seeing anything."

"Why do you need my controller? That's unsafe. It says so in the package we got."

"I just want to try something."

"Dex, the box is in the back of the drawer. But please don't do anything with it, that's unsafe."

Dexter reached his hand further back and found it, resting peacefully in its original box. He grabbed the box and opened it, pulling Juliana's controller out. "I need to try something, Jules."

"Dex, I'm driving right now."

"Jules, you can pull over."

"Dex! I'm serious. It's dark out here, and there's not really a place to pull over." Before she had the chance to say anything, her vision flashed to Dexter's before switching back. "Dex! What are you doing?"

"Who were you with tonight?" Dexter gently moved his thumb around the button on Juliana's controller.

"I was with friends! What is wrong with you?"

Dexter double-tapped the button again, waiting just a little longer for the second tap.

"Dexter, stop it!"

"Who was the guy that you were with?"

"The guy? You mean Bill, my boss? We ran into him and his wife, so they both sat down with us for a minute." Dexter wanted to believe her. "Geez, Dex, did you really spend the whole time watching what I was doing when you woke up?"

"No! It's not like that!" He double tapped the button again. He could not help himself.

"Dexter! Please stop!"

He looked down at that controller and realized that pressing her button did not fix his problem. He still saw what she saw, the windshield, the asphalt, the trees, everything on the road home. The light turned green, and Juliana continued driving.

"Dex, you have to stop this. Whatever you're feeling right now, we can talk about it when I get home."

Distress and panic fell over Dexter, both for the technological issue and for not trusting Juliana. "Jules, I think I messed up."

"I'm not sure what's happening, but let's just calm down and put the controller back."

Dexter took Juliana's controller and put it back into the box, not realizing that his finger glided against the button as he put it back. He started hearing her scream again.

"Dex! Press it again! Press it again!" I can only see your stuff!"

Realizing his mistake, Dexter frantically fumbled her controller as he pulled it from the box. But by this point, his vision had been superseded almost exclusively by Juliana's. He could not tell where the controller fell, the device sliding under the kitchen table amongst the fallen remnants of their meal earlier that day.

"Dex, I'm serious! Press the button! Press the…"

Dexter heard a loud crash on the other end of the line, followed by another crash. The phone went silent. His arms went limp, dropping his phone and the controller from his hand. He fell to the floor crying, and after a few seconds, he searched aimlessly for his phone. Once he was able to find it, he placed his finger on where the call button was, then traced to where the nine button was and held it down for several seconds. The phone started to ring.

"Nine-one-one. How may I assist you?"

"I've lost my connection."

"Excuse me, sir? What is the nature of your emergency?"

"She's gone and I can't see. I've lost my connection."

"I'm sorry, please repeat that."

"My girlfriend is dead, and I no longer have any vision."

Waiting on a Ride

"Why am I here?"

Victor Hargrove found himself on a rocking chair, sitting on the wooden porch of an old, dusty house in the middle of an even dustier field. The land was completely flat, save a few trees strewn across the landscape. "What's going on?"

"I can't tell you that." A lady called from his right side. He turned to look at her. She was beautiful. Her face looked like she could be in her forties, but her silver hair belied her youthful glow. She spoke in a sweet, songbird voice. "You have to figure that out for yourself."

"I'm not exactly sure what you mean."

"I mean what I just told you. You have to figure out what's going on, and you have to do that for yourself."

Victor scratched his salt-and-pepper beard and looked around. Between him and the beautiful woman, there was a flimsy door that swung out in only one direction. Beyond her, there were two other people sitting in wooden rocking chairs. One was a tall, full-figured older woman with long, curly gray hair, a slender face, and a bright blue dress patterned with pink flowers. The other was a tall, bald man with a sturdy and wide frame, and a beard longer than Victor's. His knuckles were dark, and he wore a blue track suit with white streaks down each side. "And what are they here for?"

The silver-haired lady turned to look at the two people to her right, then back to Victor. "I can't tell you. I can't even tell them."

Victor scrunched his face in confusion. "Then, what am I supposed to do?"

She spoke calmly with a sly smile. "Figure it out."

The lady turned her stoic face forward and stared down the empty road before us. There was nothing but flat, beige land in all directions—the road was the only distinct feature, stretching endlessly across the horizon. The man and older woman sat peacefully with their eyes closed, as if trying to recall something. With nothing to do and receiving no answers, Victor closed his eyes as well. At first, he only saw darkness. Then, light started to sift in from the background. He thought that the sun was beating down hard, but his skin was growing cold as he looked into his eyelids. Goosebumps formed along his skin and the hairs across his body started to stand up. Frigid air entered his lungs. The light in his vision intensified. Fuzzy gray humanlike forms came into his focus, but the forms had no facial features and no signifying traits—no eyes, no ears, no mouths, only flat gray. Victor opened his eyes suddenly, and took a deep, cold breath.

"What was that?" His breath quickened.

Victor's new friend kept staring across the landscape. "Hmm?"

"What was that?" he repeated. "I don't understand what's happening."

"Then you need to be patient. Just enjoy the peace."

Victor grumbled. "I can't, I need to know what's going on. Plus it's too quiet."

The lady sighed deeply and audibly, "You don't seem like the type that understands peace. Or patience, for that matter."

"That's correct. I need things to keep moving. I don't know how I got here, but I assume that I can get to where I need to be."

"And where exactly is it that you need to be?"

"I need to be at home."

"And can you tell me where your home is?"

Victor opened his mouth to respond, but he realized he could not give her a proper response. He struggled to remember where he lived, or anything else. He thought about where he lived, where he grew up, where he went to school or worked as a young man, all to no avail. But rather than feeling angry or scared, he felt nothing. No guilt about his lost memory, no shame in his inability to answer even basic questions about himself.

Before he could say anything else, the lady spoke again. "That's what I thought." He realized he must have been making faces. "I'm sure you'll eventually get it."

"Well, I do remember my name. It's Victor."

"Nice to meet you, Mr. Victor." She turned and smiled gently. "My name is Beatrice." Her skin glowed as she spoke her name. A light, cool breeze swept across the porch, making her shining silver hair dance about her shoulders. "How are you feeling?"

"Well, I'm not feeling much, actually. Still a bit confused, but remarkably calm. I don't remember being this calm at any time in my life."

"That's just wonderful. Do you remember how you normally feel?"

"Hmm... I have memories of anxiety. Lots and lots of anxiety. And a heavy weight on me. It feels like... there was always someone counting on me, and I just think about a weight on my chest, and my shoulders."

"Mmm... interesting. I've heard that from others before."

Victor was curious. "There were others?"

"Oh, of course. Many others. This place is not the only one, but many have come through this station."

"So, this is a station? Like a power station?"

"More like a bus station, except it's not just for buses."

"That means that someone is coming to pick me up?"

"Only if you're ready."

Victor did not know how to take this information. As he tried to decipher her cryptic words, a car approached from the distance. A dust cloud rose against the horizon and the unknown older lady in the blue dress with the pink flowers on the porch opened her eyes and stood up slowly, smiling from ear to ear as her hair and dress flowed in the breeze. The car moved into focus as it got closer to the station—a 1957 turquoise convertible Cadillac with whitewall tires, large and sitting low as it slowly pulled up to the porch. Despite all of the dust kicking into the air, the car rode up to the station completely clean, not a speck either on the outside or inside of the car. Victor thought it was fantastic, and clearly unreal. Even more, once the car stopped, out came another woman, the most beautiful woman he had ever seen—long, black hair with loose curls that cascaded down her back, an hourglass figure that swayed, and a flowing bright yellow dress with pink and orange flowers on it. Her red lipstick was as noticeable as the red bow in her hair. She wore white gloves and matching white high heels.

This new young woman walked up slowly and quietly, but with confidence. She was trying not to scare anyone. The unknown older woman on the porch walked down the porch stairs to meet. The young woman looked like she could be the older woman's daughter, only taller, even without her heels on. The young woman placed her hand over the older woman's heart, and a gentle orange light glowed under her hand for several seconds. Victor looked at the scene with amazement, slack-jawed and wide-eyed. After the glow dissipated, the old woman looked up at the young woman, and spoke sweetly.

"Thank you. I understand now."

The young woman replied warmly. "You're welcome. I'm glad that you understand. Are you ready to go?"

"I'm ready." The older woman started shuffling toward the car. "And thanks for bringing the car. Looks fantastic." The younger woman opened the door to the car and allowed the other to get in the backseat. Then she bent her head down and slid into the backseat as well. The door closed and the Cadillac drove away with both women waving to Beatrice, continuing down the road off into the horizon. Beatrice waved back, happy and proud.

"Wow, that was incredible." Victor remained stunned.

"Mm-hmm. It's great every time."

"Hey Beatrice, what about that other guy?" He gestured to the man on the far end of the porch with his eyes still closed.

"It depends on when he... oh, wait, here it comes."

As Beatrice spoke, the older man opened his eyes, wide and inspired. At that moment, an old-style Jeep appeared in the distance, exactly where the Cadillac first came into view earlier. It rode up to the station much faster than the Cadillac had. Despite the cloud of dust that rose around it, the Jeep—just like the Cadillac before it—appeared without a speck of dust on the body or the interior. The older man walked proudly from the porch, still moving slowly while leaning against the banister, dressed in a pair of jeans, a gray sweatshirt, and white sneakers. The Jeep stopped just as abruptly as the previous car, dust billowing from all directions. Suddenly, a young man jumped out of the Jeep wearing a crisp, green United States Army service uniform, lines sharp and shoes polished to a near-mirror shine. He wore a green beret and sported several medals and other adornments on his uniform, including a sergeant's insignia on his sleeve. He walked directly along the center of the path towards the older man. The older man did the same, albeit slower but with no less confidence. They faced each other and gave a salute. Then the younger soldier moved his saluting hand onto the older man's head. As with the young woman before, an orange glow bloomed under the young man's hand, engulfing the elder's own head in an aura of light.

"Thank you for that. I'm so happy to see you again."

"I'm glad to see you, too, old man. You've made it a long way."

"I couldn't have done it without you. Let's get going." He then turned to Beatrice and said,

"Thank you for keeping me here until it was time."

"You're welcome, sir. Thank you for being a part of it."

The young man helped the older man into the Jeep, then also joined him in the backseat. The car continued down the road with both men calmly looking out onto the new horizon.

"Beatrice, I'm still not sure what is happening."

"Well, Mr. Victor, maybe you should try closing your eyes again."

Victor closed his eyes again, looking into the darkness. Then, the gray shapes sharpened into focus. Faces slowly formed—familiar faces of people he once knew. He still could not make out who exactly they were, but it seemed as though he was starting to remember more and more. Colors and shapes were forming. He smelled citrus. He could feel that he was getting closer to the answer, but he was yanked out of focus.

"Wait, what was that?"

Beatrice looked back at him. "What was what?

"I was starting to feel something while my eyes were closed, but I heard a loud pop, and then the chairs started rocking."

"Ah yes, that was our new friend here." Beatrice leaned back to show Victor the young lady that seemed to have appeared out of thin air. She was in her late teenage years, with black shoulder-length hair. She was wearing a black corset over a long-sleeved mesh shirt that matched her skin tone, along with jeans and chunky boots. She was also wearing several bracelets, as well as gloves with the fingers cut below her knuckles.

"How did she get there?"

"Beats me. People tend to come whenever it's time for them to come, and they go when it's time for them to go. How that happens, I don't know and I don't ask questions."

"But you've seen lots of people come and go at this station?"

"That's right."

"And is it normal for people to just appear out of nowhere?"

"As I said, Mr. Victor, I don't know. People come out of the station, or around the corner on this porch, or fall from the sky. How they get here is not really any of my business." Her calmness never wavered. "Once, I had a guy roll from the top of this roof. Fell right in front of me without any warning. He picked himself up, arranged his suit jacket and tie, and then he sat in one of these chairs waiting to figure out when his ride was coming, just like everyone else."

"You were never curious?"

"Not at all. I don't feel any sort of curiosity toward the people that come my way. All I do is try to make a nice, calm space for folks to rest and wait for their ride. I'm not here to poke at anyone, and I'm not here to judge. I'm here to make sure everyone feels safe."

Victor did feel safe. Her easy conversation was soothing. Still, it did not help him figure out why he was there. He closed his eyes again, but this time there was more than darkness. It all started with the gray shadows floating in front of him. The citrus smell returned, and now there were specks of red forming—the stripes of someone's tie, a baseball cap, some fuzzy wires in in the distance. Then came orange and yellow colors—prisms near the bottom of his view, circles floating in front and above him, the outline of a bright shirt upon one of the faceless gray figures.

Are these people I know?

Again, as things started to take shape and focus, he heard the faint sound of a bicycle bell in the distance. He opened his eyes and saw a little girl with dirty blonde pigtails and a powder-blue dress ride along the road. There was a large two-wheeled basket attached to the back of her bike, like a makeshift wagon to the rear axle. The little girl eased to a stop in front of the station, as all arrivals did. The older girl walked down the steps towards her.

Victor was impressed. "Well, that was fast."

Beatrice answered. "Yeah, I've noticed that before. The younger they are, the quicker they seem to go. I think they're able to figure things out faster, since they don't have much to hold them up from leaving."

Victor remained confused.

The little girl ran to the teenager and gave her a big hug. The older girl hugged her back before the younger took hold of her wrists. A familiar orange glow emitted from beneath the teenager's gloves, and once the light waned, she took them off.

"I'm glad you were the one to do it."

The little girl responded. "I'm sorry it happened. I'm just glad we were able to see each other again."

"Me too. I'm ready now."

198

The little girl ran to the bicycle and jumped on the seat. The teenager sat in the basket on the back, tucking her arms and feet in as the little girl rang her bell. Victor thought it looked silly. Again, Beatrice did not waver. They both turned and waved at Victor and Beatrice and shouted, "Thank you!" in unison. Beatrice and Victor waved as they rode off just as all the others had.

"Okay, Beatrice. I need to figure out how this works."

"Mr. Victor, as I've said already, I cannot help you. You will have to get to this on your own."

He closed his eyes again. The forms, the faces, the colors—everything came flooding back. The citrus scent was starting to mix with the smell of iron. He started to hear sounds—timid laughter mixed with faint crying, and then he felt drops of water plopping against his hand. Finally, the images started to differentiate more clearly. Lights above, people around him, holding his hand. He could not tell who they were, but he could tell that they knew him.

But again, his focus was disrupted by the sound of two diesel engines roaring in the distance. As he looked up, he saw two yellow school buses racing down. As the buses came to a stop in front of the house, a group of elementary school children ran through the door out onto the porch in a single file. Victor surmised there were around thirty-five children, each with parts of their clothing torn. There were battered shirts, ripped pants, some even had holes in their shoes. The buses pulled up and the children ran out, one by one, to greet and hug a child onboard the buses waiting for them. As the children hugged, the same faint orange light glowed between each pair. Once the children all found their places, they opened their windows, waved, and yelled an excited "Goodbye!" to those at the station. But Victor noticed something strange. For each child that boarded the bus with tattered clothing, there was another child identical to them, down to their clothing. The only difference was that the children already on the bus wore clothes that were perfectly clean and fresh, with no apparent tears or holes. To Victor the children had found a friend in their own selves for their journey. Victor smiled and waved back, then looked at Beatrice's forlorn smile before closing his eyes again.

The people around him were in focus now. One woman with salt-and-pepper hair was holding his hand and crying over him as he was laying down.

Those tears must have been what I felt against my hand before.

The lights were bright and white, and they hummed softly. He could see light blue tiling across the ground. He realized the citrus smell was artificial, most likely from the cleaning supplies used to sanitize the space.

We're in a hospital.

He felt the mask against his face and the tube down his throat, and he started to gag.

I'm on some kind of support machine.

The colors that were once fuzzy became clear—his brother's bright Hawaiian shirt and shiny watch, his sister's rich purple dress and the gold crucifix hanging from her neck, his young nephew's white shirt and floral shorts, his wife's blue jeans and dark blue blouse with the bracelet he had given her for their thirty-fifth anniversary. He felt her hand stroking his. He caught a whiff of her lavender perfume, and he felt the diamond of her engagement ring against his palm as she occasionally and nervously twisted it around her fingers with her thumb. He felt his organs struggle, but he did not feel any pain.

Multiple organ failure. They must have me on morphine or something.

He could see his family speaking, but he could not hear them. His hearing was starting to fade. As quickly as he had started to see colors, they started to fade, desaturating with each passing moment.

This is the end.

He understood where he was now.

I'm at the end.

He opened his eyes to see Beatrice looking at him, grinning the biggest grin that he'd seen on her face since he arrived at the station porch. At that moment, Beatrice turned her head toward the horizon, where a beat-up old sedan had appeared. It was the first car that Victor ever purchased with his own money—a 1986 Montreal Blue Honda Accord. The memory of working small jobs around his neighborhood and at the grocery store just to afford the down payment came back to him. He felt again the sense of accomplishment that he had felt driving it around, knowing how hard he had worked to afford it. The car pulled up, and out came a seventeen-year-old boy from the driver's seat. It was his younger self, full of all the pride and joy he had felt when he bought that car.

"I get it now." He walked down the porch steps as the younger Victor walked forward to meet him. "It's been a while since I've even thought about this car."

"I know. It was a fun time for us."

"The best time." Victor reached out for a handshake, but the younger Victor opened his arms for a hug. Victor opened his arms and they embraced. Victor could not see the glow surrounding him, but as he closed his eyes, memories from his life flooded back to him.

The first girl he kissed.

His first job as a drafter at an architecture firm.

His last day at his first job when he told off his boss for how poorly he had been treated.

The beginning of his new job as the owner of a diner.

Meeting the woman at his first diner that later became his wife.

The birth and loss of his child.

The joy of helping raise his brother's children.

The vacations and birthdays and anniversaries and graduations and marriages and funerals and all of the things that had made his life worth living.

He also felt everything inside him working again. He had not realized how empty he had been until he was embraced by his younger self—his best self. He took a deep breath and felt a sense of peace overwhelm him. He exhaled and started to cry.

"Thank you so much for coming to get me."

"You're welcome. I'm glad we are able to do this together. Are you ready to go?"

He looked back at Beatrice, still with tears in his eyes, and smiled at her. She smiled back and gave a gentle, polite wave. "I'm ready."

Victor turned and walked proudly and slowly to the car. Rather than getting in the back, he entered the driver's door.

"Are you sure you want to do that?" Younger Victor was concerned.

"I'm not all-the-way gone yet. I want to feel this one last time."

"Sounds like a good plan, old man." Younger Victor walked around the car and slid into the front passenger side. Older Victor relaxed into the driver's seat, feeling the soft fabric against his back.

"Feels like it was just yesterday."

He looked out at Beatrice one last time and mouthed, "Thank you," before putting his foot on the gas pedal. Beatrice murmured, "You're welcome," to herself and watched as they rode away together. Victor looked out onto the horizon, thinking about his life and lamenting how many of those that he saw today had never gotten to live as full a life as he had. But he was proud of what he had done with the time that he had had. He knew, as the others had known before him, that there was more to come.

Acknowledgements

Thank you.

I want to thank my editor, Sheeba Arif, for her hard work in ensuring that this collection of short stories communicate my ideas effectively and with the appropriate care.

I want to thank my cover artist, Chloe Arzuaga, for her consistency and ability to display the vision for this collection and for my first novella, *The Ghosts of Poplar Valley*.

I want to thank the editor of my first novella, Wendy Muruli, who provided the first professional review of my first novella and gave me the confidence to pursue storytelling. I didn't think to include my acknowledgement publicly to her, so I would like to remedy that.

I want to thank Hajar Moutawakkil and Soukayna Jamali for helping with my Arabic.

I want to thank the Prince George's County Public School System in Prince George's County, Maryland, for providing the educational foundation for my work and career.

I want to thank all of the family, friends, acquaintances, and others that I have come across in my life who supported me in my artistic endeavors and, in some cases, inspired my work.

Finally, I want to thank you, the reader, for taking your precious time to read this work. It means a lot to me.

If you are moved to do so, feel free to do the following:

Review this book publicly by posting your rating and thoughts on Amazon or Goodreads.
Recommend this book to your family, friends, and colleagues.
Support other independent authors by purchasing their books.

And if you really liked this collection, please purchase my first novella, *The Ghosts of Poplar Valley*, available in print and on Kindle.